EMBER IN SPACE BOOK ONE

*USA TODAY* BESTSELLING AUTHOR

# REBECCA RODE

**Getting sold to the Empire was never part of the plan.**

Ember lives two very different lives. By day she's a mysterious Roma future-teller, and by night she struggles to care for her sick father. All she wants is the power to control her own life—no arranged marriage, no more poverty. Her future-reading talent is what will get her there.

But when the Empire discovers her gift, Ember's life changes forever.

Ember soon finds her innocent talent is far more dangerous than she believed. The Empire wants to turn her into a deadly weapon. But Ember has plans of her own, and they don't include living under the Empire's control.

Because even the best weapons can backfire.

*For my fiercely independent four*

# 1

Ember ran her fingers absently along the faded purple tablecloth and brushed away a stray crumb. She hadn't had time for laundry this morning, and it desperately needed scrubbing. Today's customers would just have to deal with it.

She didn't have time for laundry in general these days. Tourist season meant sitting at her market stall during daylight hours, smiling at visitors as they glared back, and offering to read their futures as they made their way down to the beach. And worrying about her sleeping father at home, of course. She'd planted a kiss on her Dai's feverish forehead and had come early today, hoping to catch the first wave of tourists before the other sellers arrived and scared them off.

The smuggler would be here with Dai's medicine any day now, and she was well short of his price. She couldn't afford to miss a single customer.

Today's shuttle, docked in the distance, was small and unfamiliar—a CVL-2078, passenger limit eighty-two. Its passengers barely shot her a glance as they pranced excitedly from the dock toward the warm sand, their trim bodies carefully sculpted as if they had nothing useful to do wherever it was they'd come from.

These tourists would be great-grandchildren of the original exodus. Most of them had never been back to Earth their entire life. Earth was a dead thing now, a historical monument to the beginning of the human race. Only the Roma remained, making a living from the scraps everyone else had left behind. For nearly a century, their only visitors had been scientists and historians—until a celebrity declared their beach the best in three galaxies. Now they had plenty of business.

As long as the tourists kept returning with their chips full of credits, Ember wasn't going to complain.

She eyed the sky, which was only a slightly lighter shade of brown than the last time she checked. Twenty minutes, maybe thirty, and she'd go home and make sure Dai ate. She swallowed back the guilt, knowing he'd be lying awake in bed by now, hungry and missing his daughter. She should have forced him to eat before she left. But his nights of sound and painless sleep were few and far between these days.

She smoothed her scowl into a more pleasant expression as another group of tourists approached. This group ignored the sellers' calls completely, seeming intensely interested in the packed dirt road at their feet.

"Shoes," the shoemaker called out two stalls down. "Half price for you." His accent was atrocious. The man spoke just enough Common to sell the occasional pair of plastic shoes he'd marked up three times their worth. Ember had once offered to teach him more of the language, but he'd scoffed at the offer. Not that she cared. If he wanted to sound ridiculous at the market, it was his business.

"Love, prosperity," Ember said to a blonde woman whose rolls bulged beneath her thin swimsuit. "Give me five minutes, and I will reveal what awaits you."

The lady's eyes grew wide as she took in Ember's traditional blouse and long skirt. Then she shook her head so violently Ember worried the woman would fall right over.

"He said there would be gypsies," her companion muttered to her, and they shared a knowing look. Then they strode down the walk arm in arm, ignoring the other sellers' offers.

Ember sighed. Their pilot must have issued a warning to his passengers. There wouldn't be any business today.

She carefully gathered her mother's cards. They were soft from use, the back sides hand-painted by another Roma future-teller long ago, although she'd never asked her mother who. She'd waited too long to ask, and now she'd never know.

She slipped them into her hidden skirt pocket and began to fold her tablecloth. She'd come back later, as the tourists returned to their shuttle. Maybe they'd be less uptight then. And if not, she'd have to be more aggressive with her price. The smuggler wouldn't give her Dai's medicine without full payment. That she knew from experience.

Movement in the sky caught her attention, and she paused. A streak of light descended from the sky toward the landing field. Another shuttle. Ember could barely remember the last time their small coastal town had hosted so many tourists at once. Usually several days passed between groups.

She threw a quick glance in the direction of her village. Surely Dai could wait a few more minutes. If she left now, she'd miss the next group completely. Besides, their supper would consist of yesterday's leftover bread and an old tomato. One customer, maybe two, and she could afford to pay the smuggler *and* buy some meat for dinner.

Ember spread the tablecloth once again and retrieved her cards, seating herself on the edge of her chair. The other sellers had noticed the incoming shuttle as well and hurriedly straightened their wares, even though it wasn't needed. The one exception was the seed woman directly across the aisle from Ember. She sat in her usual hunched position, patiently holding her open bag of sunflower seeds. Her face was barely visible beneath the handkerchief covering the braid that indicated she was a married woman. The woman had been dozing practically since Ember's childhood.

The new ship docked a respectable distance past the other shuttle. Ember had to stand to see it over the market's assortment of makeshift walls. The shuttle appeared large and shiny enough to be encouraging, although she couldn't quite make out the model. It was slightly more rounded, which meant it was newer than most. But one thing gave her pause.

The Empire's silver-and-blue banner glimmered across the craft's hull.

Ember swallowed, her stomach fluttering nervously. Empire ships didn't often come here, and when they did—well, it was an uncomfortable matter for the Roma. The soldiers seemed to have no purpose but to look for infractions and hunt down those who hadn't paid homage.

It had been months since Ember had paid hers. She only had nineteen credits left. If the soldiers decided they wanted it, it would set Ember back several weeks. Not to mention Dai wouldn't get his medicine. Again. She didn't want to consider what would happen to him if he went another month without his pills.

*Please be tourists and not soldiers.*

It was nearly another half hour before the new visitors trickled in. Ember scanned the crowd and breathed a relieved sigh. Not a single silver uniform in sight. If they were soldiers, they were vacationing today.

These tourists were more relaxed and less hurried than the others. Sauntering between the stalls and tables and examining the wares, they looked fascinated by the market and its dark-skinned sellers. A small group of younger visitors—in their twenties, she guessed—stayed together in the center of the aisle and whispered, but it appeared to be an exchange of friendly information, not judgment on her people in general.

One of them, a man who looked to be only slightly older than Ember, caught her watching and smiled. He stood taller than the rest, his gray shirt pulled tight against his broad shoulders. His skin was light, as with most *gadje,* though his hair was nearly as dark as hers. Thick, black eyebrows framed his nearly transparent-gray eyes.

She felt her cheeks warm. She wasn't supposed to find *gadje* attractive. Then again, her own company, or *kumpania*, thought there was something wrong with her. Few women reached sixteen, much less Ember's nineteen years, unmarried. Most had a child by now. Her friend Bianca had a son, with another babe expected any day.

Ember mingled with the outsiders and took their money, but she had drawn a solid, uncrossable line no matter how attractive the outsider. Tradition was important above all because tradition kept them safe. It was the Roma creed.

She tapped her cards on the table. "Know your future," she called to the man. "Five minutes, and I will reveal what awaits you."

Surprise registered in his face, and then his grin broadened.

"Did you hear that, Stefan?" the petite girl at his side said with a musical laugh as she elbowed him in the ribs. "The gypsy girl wants to tell your fortune." She wore a strappy blue dress that hung low over the bust and barely covered her rear end. Her light hair was streaked with blue to match, although Ember suspected the streaks were temporary.

"My future, eh?" he asked, thoughtfully tapping his chin. He finally nodded and made his way over to Ember's stall.

"You can't be serious," the girl said.

"I'm serious if she is." He settled himself in the chair. "What do you charge, gypsy?"

"Fifty credits."

He entered the amount into his wristband with its approval code and extended his arm for her to scan. Ember quickly raised her own and intercepted the money, the wristband beeping as the transaction went through.

"Stefan, you're not actually paying this—this *thief* to tell your future," the girl snapped, glowering at Ember. "I could do it in thirty seconds."

"I'm just curious, Eris. Get off my back," Stefan said, then turned back to Ember expectantly. "You know what? If you impress me, I'll triple your price."

Ember knew she was gaping and hurriedly smoothed her face. *One hundred and fifty credits.* "Very well, but I'll need silence from your friends." She shot a pointed look at the blonde girl, Eris. The girl snapped her mouth shut, her cheeks going pink.

The street leading to the beach was filling with spectators now, most of whom seemed to know Stefan. Some looked impatient, but most watched with amused chuckles. Good. Entertained crowds meant good business and the occasional tip. *Three times her price.* She hadn't gotten an offer like that before, ever.

Ember separated her cards, closed her eyes, and began to sway. She ignored the snickers that peppered the crowd and hummed a song under her breath as she spread the cards in front of her. Customers usually focused on the pictures, but the cards were just for show. The real magic took place within her.

Ember reached out, inwardly searching for the man's inner light. She found it immediately—a flickering light, much like a flame. His soul was slightly dim since he was calm and relaxed, but it warmed her as she drew nearer to it and mentally grasped it.

*The maze of walls extended as far as Stefan could see. Metal slabs stood tall and cold, littered with thousands of names. Stefan was only twelve, but he'd already been here three times—for his grandfather, his aunt, and now his older brother.*

*He tugged at his uniform before returning his gaze to the ground. It felt strange to stand with his parents and not have Adam here making fun of the well-wishers as they streamed past. Their expressions were serious and seemed genuine enough, but most had never even met Adam. They were just friends of his parents, ready to cross "pay respects" off their list.*

*"What an incredible sacrifice," a plump man said. He stood a full foot shorter than Stefan's father. "You must be so proud of your son."*

*"We are," Stefan's mother said. "His heroic death has honored us."*

*Stefan flinched. It was like he wasn't even there.*

*"I'm sure the emperor holds your family in the highest esteem," the man continued. "I hope you won't mourn long, especially with another flicker in the family." The visitor nodded to Stefan, but the man's expression held no warmth. "Maybe you'll make it to Empyrean someday after all."*

*"I suppose there's always a chance," Stefan's father said, looking upon his younger son, but the words were strained.*

Ember pulled away and opened her eyes, settling her gaze on the customer. This older version of Stefan had stronger features and far more confidence. He watched her with what appeared to be curiosity, but she could still see a glimmer of emotion in his eyes, that inner pain from years before. He still suffered his brother's loss, however well he tried to conceal it.

But that was the past. What this man wanted was the future. Ironically, most customers didn't really want the truth but something to cling to. A hope. Ember sensed that wasn't the case with this man. It was important to him that she get this right.

She reconnected mentally and moved toward the end of the man's memories, pushing ever forward. When the memories ended, the light extended slightly, indicating these events hadn't been fulfilled yet. The future. One particular scene pulsed brighter than the rest, and she plunged into the light.

*Stefan stepped forward and saluted. He stood stone-still while an officer placed a pin on his uniform collar, the same pin his brother had once worn. It weighed far more than the .06 ounces it was supposed to. He was an official flicker now. This was exactly what he'd always wanted, but it felt empty somehow. Hollow. Meaningless.*

*He stepped back in line. Someone patted him on the back, but it felt like consolation, not pride.*

Ember pulled out and opened her eyes. Stefan watched her carefully, his smile bemused. He probably assumed she was making something up to scam him out of his money.

"You want to break out of your brother's shadow," Ember finally said. "But it won't bring you the happiness you crave."

Stefan blinked in surprise.

"What kind of fortune is that?" the Eris girl exclaimed with a snicker. "I don't think you even know what fortune-telling is, gypsy girl."

"Wait," Stefan said, still stunned. He raised a hand to still the muttering crowd. "You've got to give me more than that." He leaned toward Ember, his gaze so intense she couldn't look away if she'd wanted to. "Be more specific, and I'll quadruple your price. That's two hundred credits."

*Two hundred.* Her mind ran through the possibilities. She could pay for her father's medicine with money to spare. They'd eat like kings for a week. Her stomach grumbled, reminding her she hadn't eaten since yesterday.

He expectantly held out his wristband, and Ember accepted the higher payment, feeling dazed.

Movement caught her eye as a group in silver uniforms made

their way down the aisle toward her. Ember's heart sank. Definitely soldiers. One had an unusually large chin, and his black uniform was littered with colorful patches and ribbons. His build, chiseled and hard, was the type that required hours of work each week. One look at the man's eyes made Ember shiver.

The crowd parted to let them through. The man in black led his soldiers straight for her, then they stopped behind Stefan as if to watch.

Panic rose inside her. Did this man know she hadn't paid homage? Would they take any money she earned today?

She forced herself to breathe normally, to think clearly. If she had to, she'd pay homage out of the two hundred credits. She'd still have just enough for Dai's medicine.

Ember took a deep breath and closed her eyes, feeling the weight of two dozen eyes on her. Once again, she reached out internally and plunged into the light.

*Ember stared at him with her lips slightly parted, her beautiful, dark eyes wide in surprise. A strand of her wild black hair hung over face, and he longed to brush it aside. But he didn't dare, not until he knew how she felt.*

*"Did you—" he began, but she didn't give him a chance to continue. She threaded her fingers into his hair and pulled him downward, pressing her lips to his.*

*He grinned against her lips and placed his hand on the small of her back, pulling her against him. He'd longed for this for weeks, and now here she was, making the first move. He deepened the kiss, and she responded until his head went dizzy. He could hardly bear the heat jumping between them.*

*Someone walking by hooted, as if they were just another couple. Two soldiers about to embark on a battle, just two people from completely different galaxies whose futures were forever intertwined.*

Ember yanked herself out of the vision and shot out of her chair. It fell to the dirt with a sharp *thump*. She gasped for air, looking at the crowd with an edge of panic. They watched her with interest now, obviously unsure why she'd stopped her humming and card shuffling so dramatically. Her mother's cards were strewn haphazardly across the table. Some had even fallen to the ground.

"I—" She cleared her throat and tried to smile, but she knew it was shaky. "I'm sorry, but there's nothing else."

# 2

The crowd was silent for a moment. Stefan's face registered shock.

The girl named Eris burst out with a bitter laugh. "I told you, Stefan, didn't I? She's an actress. Gypsies are all the same. Let's go to the beach now." She whirled and headed toward the sleeping woman with the sunflower seeds.

"I will return your money." Ember typed in the amount and held out her arm. Her hand trembled slightly.

Stefan was still watching her carefully, his eyes narrowed in suspicion. "You're sure you didn't see something?"

"The stars are silent." Her voice broke on the last word, and she cleared her throat.

He nodded slowly, as if Ember had confirmed something in his mind. Then he stood. "Keep it."

Stefan turned and crossed the street to follow Eris. When he reached her, they began what looked like a heated argument. Normally Ember would be curious to know the details of their exchange. It almost looked like he was defending Ember. But she was too numb to do anything but stand and watch . . . and think.

Ember had never questioned her gift before. Her visions were just too detailed to be made up by her subconscious, and most of her repeat business reported that her predictions had come true. But this? The stars had to be playing a twisted joke on her. How could she kiss that . . . that . . . *gadjo*? Not just kiss him, but throw herself at him in a most un-Roma way.

The market tilted and swayed around her. She kicked her chair upright and plopped into it again, remembering the way they'd looked at each other in her vision. It wasn't just the excitement of a new relationship or the possibility of a future together. He'd seen her as something precious—like she was everything that mattered to him. And she had kissed him with an openness, a complete trust she'd never experienced before. And there was *something else* hovering between them during the kiss, something Ember still detected in her father's eyes whenever he looked at her mother's photograph.

Love.

She shook her head. Her gift had betrayed her. That man would climb back onto his ship and go back to wherever he'd come from, and Ember would go home and care for her father. Eventually, when her father was better and didn't need her anymore, she'd fall in love with a respectable Rom man. She'd forget about the outsider by next week.

She had enough money for Dai's medicine now. The next bottle would last him two more months—plenty of time to recover. This was definitely her day.

As the crowd dispersed, the officer stepped forward. "My turn."

Her stomach plummeted. She'd forgotten about the soldiers. Ember's heart threatened to pound right out of her chest as she faced the man. Her instincts were shouting at her now, telling her to get away. She could hear sounds of fumbling with boxes and hurried preparations coming from the other stalls. Of course. The other sellers had already begun to pack up at the sight of an officer. She should be doing the same thing, yet she sat here, frozen.

"Um . . ." she began. "Are you a homage officer?"

"No, no. Nothing like that. Just curious about my future." Her unwelcome guest sat himself in the chair Stefan had just vacated. His four guards—three men and a disturbingly tall woman with pink hair—surrounded him, eyeing her like prey. The officer programmed the payment into his wristband and extended his arm.

Ember didn't dare breathe. Officers never wanted their futures read. Ember had always assumed it was because they already knew what awaited them—a lifetime of killing ended by an abrupt and violent death. Dai had been an Empire soldier before joining the Roma, and he refused to talk about his experiences. It must have been a terrible thing for a human being to fight in battle, particularly one as kindhearted as Dai.

No, Empire soldiers didn't like their futures told. That meant this man had another reason for his request. She couldn't imagine what it would be.

*Something is wrong,* her heart told her. *Get out of here.*

"I will pay double your fee," the officer said. He brought his wristband closer so she could verify the amount on the screen. It was a fancy, lightweight model she'd never seen before.

"Ember!" a frantic voice called from behind her.

"Bianca?" Ember turned to find her friend coming down the road from their village. Bianca was breathing hard and holding her back as if in pain. She didn't often descend the hill these days, not with the birth so close at hand. Her news had to be urgent.

"Your dai needs you," Bianca said in broken Common. "You must come right now." Her eyes flicked to the officer, and she swallowed hard, staring at the ground.

Ember's panic began to dissolve. If it had been a true emergency, her friend would have been far more frantic and spouted off in Romani. Bianca had obviously seen the officer and decided to rescue her. Dear friend.

"Forgive me, sir." Ember swept her mother's cards into her hand, then quickly bent to retrieve the ones that had fallen into the dirt. She pulled the tablecloth into a bundle in her arms, exposing the ugly table underneath. She didn't have time to carry the chairs today. She'd have to risk them getting stolen.

The officer's eyes narrowed, all pretense gone. "What is your family name, Ember gypsy? Are there others like you?"

"Gheorghe, sir." She paused. "I'm the only one who reads the cards." She didn't actually need the cards to read a person's future, but she wasn't about to tell the officer that. Dai was the only one who knew about her strange gift, and even he seemed ashamed, forbidding her to discuss it with anyone. Not even Bianca knew specifics.

Her answer seemed to please the officer, though she couldn't imagine why. A strange glint entered his eye. "How did you know about that man's brother? A lucky guess?"

Her heart pounded against her ribs. All Roma knew how dangerous soldiers could be, and this was an Empire officer. She was required by law to answer his questions. Which would be worse, saying she was a liar or admitting she had a gift?

"I must go," she finally said, her throat tight. "My father is ill. I'm very sorry."

He gave her a long, searching look. Finally he spoke. "I will allow you to leave on one condition. You will return tonight at sunset. Be on time, or I will come looking for you, and believe me, that will be rather unpleasant. Understood, Ember Gheorghe?"

He'd arranged her name in the Common way, but she didn't point it out. "Yes, sir."

The officer looked her up and down for a moment, and stories of soldiers claiming Roma women, then leaving them with child flooded through her mind. Her dark hair was unbraided, flying free to signify she was a maiden. Did this man know what it meant? Was that the cause of his inexplicable interest?

"Go," he finally said.

Ember didn't hesitate. She grabbed Bianca's arm and pulled her along toward the hill.

An officer. Earth hadn't seen an Empire officer in over a decade—and now one had issued her an order. She had no desire to return, but dared she defy him? Especially since Bianca was now involved.

Maybe he really did want to know his future. Ember couldn't bear to think of the alternative.

Bianca loosened up a bit as they walked, making jokes as if nothing had happened, but Ember's mind was elsewhere.

She felt the officer's eyes on her back long after the market was out of sight.

# 3

He looked even meaner up close," Bianca said as they walked.

Ember let her shoulders slouch a bit now that the village loomed before them. Hundreds of cinderblock homes stood on either side of the dirt road. Most were simple cubes with a small outdoor courtyard for cooking, but occasionally there was an actual glass window. Ember's home had once boasted two before the village children smashed them.

"I owe you," Ember said. "How did you know about the officer?"

"Mimi sent me to the market. She's *sick*." She emphasized the word with a grin. Bianca's mother-in-law was frequently drunk and spent much of her time in bed. As one of the older and therefore more respected women in their kumpania, Mimi took full advantage of her status. "Dretta's son walked by and said an officer was lingering at your stall. Who else would help but me?"

Too true. The other Roma tolerated her, but they would never come to her rescue like that. Not with her *gadjo* father and traitorous mother. She leaned over and gave her friend a peck on the cheek in gratitude. "Thank the stars for you. I haven't seen you in days. I was beginning to think Mimi tied you up in a corner somewhere."

"The life of a boria is lovely but hard." Her smile faltered just a bit as she slowed, clutching her rounded belly. "Someday you'll experience it yourself."

Ember already knew more about marriage than she wanted to. First the ceremony, then moving in with the groom's family. The new bride was responsible for the laundry, cleaning, and cooking while the bori, or mother-in-law, looked on. Mimi was less rigid than most, but the woman rarely let Bianca go to the market, much less visit her shameful half-blood friend. It made this time together all the more precious.

"Where is Luca?" Ember asked. Bianca usually had her three-year-old son with her, but he was nowhere in sight.

"Playing somewhere outside. I'll walk you home and then go find him. The soldiers aren't coming here, right? I only saw four of them."

"I don't think so. Their shuttle was mostly tourists." That part was strange. She couldn't decipher why they'd be traveling together on an Empire ship. The military had their own craft.

The officer wanted her back by sunset. Surely the Empire ship was leaving shortly afterward. How long would the man wait for her? Would he even have time to search her out in the village? There had to be other future-readers in the galaxy, if that was what he really wanted. And there were plenty of women to please him in other ways. It was all so odd.

"How is your dai?" Bianca asked, pulling her out of her thoughts. "Has the smuggler come yet?"

"No. It's been a week since Ambrose said he would come. Maybe he'll be there tonight." She couldn't hide the worry in her voice. Ember didn't know of any other smugglers who came to the outer planets, and the healer had no idea what ailed Dai. None of the woman's prescriptions ever helped. If only they had a hospital here. The closest one was on Enceladus, a day's journey by shuttle. And an expensive trip, at that. The entire kumpania could pool their money and still not have a quarter of the fare.

Bianca shook her head. "Well, I brought you this, hoping I'd find you at the market." She handed Ember a brown bag.

Ember took it and peeked inside. A piece of stringy ewe meat, a tomato, and some figs.

"Bianca!" she burst out. "Don't tell me you're stealing from Mimi again."

"I didn't steal it. We came across some good business recently with the horses. We can't spare much, but at least it's something. Tell your dai Gavril and I asked after him."

"We don't need help. We're doing just fine."

Ember tried to give it back, but Bianca raised her hands. "Do you think I'm stupid? Just take it and don't think so much about it."

Ember frowned, resentment spreading through her chest like acid. Months ago it would have been Ember giving charity. Her father had just sent off his first shipment of furniture when the sickness settled in his lungs. Now all his orders were being canceled as his customers found what they wanted elsewhere. Once he recovered, it would take a year or two to rebuild his business.

*Why couldn't you have sent me a practical gift?* she asked the stars. *Like furniture making.*

"Thanks," she muttered, wrapping the bag up and tucking it under her arm.

Bianca's hand lifted to her swollen stomach, and she grimaced. "Gavril thinks I will give him another son, but I think it's a *chey*. This one is too sharp with her kicks."

They reached Ember's home. It looked much like the others, only slightly larger and sporting square holes where the window-panes had once been. Hens squawked from the courtyard beyond. Ember had neglected to feed them this morning, too.

"Well, thanks again. I hope I see you again soon." Ember turned away.

"Wait." Bianca stared at the ground. "I've been meaning to ask you about something. Gavril talked to Coste the other day."

"Please don't," Ember broke in, too tired to argue about this again. "I know you mean well, but I can't discuss it right now."

"You can spare one minute, Ember. Is it true you refused him? Tell me it's not true. Not after everything he's done for you, the times he has defended you—"

Ember snorted. "All the times? Coste stopped the children from calling me 'old maid' once, Bianca. It hardly qualifies as gallantry."

"He offered a bride price for you. Do you understand how rare that is?"

"Of course I do." She knew better than most, actually. The sharp pangs of a dark, painful memory emerged, but Ember shoved them back. Now wasn't the time to dwell on that terrible night. "Most guys don't even bother. They just kidnap the girls they want. Cheapen them first, then get them for free."

Bianca flinched as her face fell.

A horrible realization struck Ember then. "No. You're not serious."

"I can't believe you just figured it out. It's been four years since we married, Ember."

She was right. Ember should have known. Bianca's words felt like a well-deserved slap to the face. "But you looked so happy at your *plotchka*. I thought you wanted to marry him. How could you not tell me?"

"Oh, like you told me what happened the night your mom died?"

Ember paused. "That's not fair." She hadn't confided in Bianca about her mother's death, true. But nobody knew the truth. Except Dai, perhaps, but he wasn't talking about it either.

How could she explain something she didn't quite understand herself?

"Not fair?" Bianca turned to go, her cheeks stained with pink. "All you can see are your own cares, your own suffering. You're not the only one with problems."

"I didn't mean to hurt you, Bianca."

Her friend turned back to face her. "Nobody in their right mind would marry you now, Ember. You pretend not to see it, but you know what they say about you. You're barren or unclean. Some even say cursed. And yet Coste ignored all of it and asked anyway. His family offered more than they should to help with your dai's medicines. And you threw it back in his face, just like with the others."

It wasn't exactly true. Coste had offered a bride price, yes. But she hadn't rejected him in a cruel way. She'd just . . . explained things to him. Told him she couldn't leave Dai. Said she had to stay until he was better. She could still remember the anger in Coste's expression. He hadn't understood. In his eyes, as in everyone's, Coste was doing her a favor.

Apparently Bianca didn't understand either.

"Dai needs me," Ember said. "I can't abandon him. I'm all he has."

"He doesn't need you," Bianca said flatly. "He needs money. Medicine. Proper medical care. You can't give that to him, not on tourist gratuities." She paused and her voice grew soft. "And if you keep running from those who would help you, you'll be even more ostracized than you are now. I know Coste isn't that much better than Babik, but you can bet he's your last chance. Stop being stupid and ask him if he'll take you back."

In her eyes it was simple. For Ember it was anything but. As the daughter of a Roma woman and a *gadjo,* however liked and accepted he was by her tribe, she had been an outsider at birth. Her parents raised her Roma, but in her dealings with friends and boyfriends there had always been that hesitation, that reluctance to fully accept her.

To the *gadje* she was a gypsy. To her people it was the other way around.

How could Ember explain what her parents once had? The way they treated each other with such tenderness? They'd truly liked one another. They took on traditional roles, but they did it as a gift to one another. He cared for her and brought home money. She prepared his favorite meals and kept his home for him. And at night they talked and laughed as if they'd waited all day to be together again.

That was before. Now she was gone, and Dai wasn't doing well. And as long as Ember was the only thing standing between him and the last good-bye, she refused to stand down.

"Thanks for the concerns, but you have plenty of your own." She brushed Bianca's protruding stomach and leaned over to speak to her friend's unborn child. "Grow well, dear one. Be kind to your mother."

Bianca frowned, but her anger was already fading. "I have to go now, before Mimi wakes up. Love is just a *gadjo* notion, one your dai should never have planted in your mind. Just think about it, all right?"

Luca, Bianca's energetic three-year-old, came bounding up to them. He barely gave Ember a glance, turning instead to his mother. "I'm hungry."

Bianca gave Ember an apologetic smile. "I'll try to slip away again soon. Be careful."

Ember nodded, knowing her friend referred to the officer. She still had several hours to decide what to do. In the meantime, it was time to check on Dai.

~

When her friend was out of sight, Ember pushed the makeshift door open and entered. She passed through the living area with its assortment of mismatched chairs all arranged neatly at the table in the way her mother preferred. She missed sitting there for meals. It had been so long.

She knocked gently on her father's doorframe and swept the divider cloth aside.

He lay just as she'd left him, but his eyes were open now, his expression clouded with pain. Dai still only took up half the bed, as if subconsciously leaving an empty space for a wife who would never return. He blinked at the sight of Ember, like she'd roused him from a daydream. "You're back early. How was business?"

"Good," she said, hoping he wouldn't press the matter. "How is the pain today?"

"Nothing I can't handle."

Ember knew that was a lie. Sometimes the pain in his chest grew so intense he trembled and wept like a babe. Even now his eyes pulled tight like he was trying to hide his usual grimace.

Tonight, she promised herself. She'd wait until the Empire ship was gone, then sneak down to the hollow behind Talpa's home to meet the smuggler. If Ambrose still wasn't there, she'd start asking around for another source. There had to be someone else in the sector with the pills she needed.

Ember forced a smile. "We'll have meat tonight. What do you think of that?"

"I think it sounds fantastic. Anything unusual today?"

"Nothing out of the ordinary," she lied, retrieving a fig from her bag. Half the village could be dying of a plague, and she would tell him the exact same thing. As cautious as her people were about the Empire soldiers, Dai was the most extreme in his hatred. He refused to allow Ember anywhere near them. If he knew she'd spoken with an officer today, it would kill him. She was smarter than that.

She handed him the fig. "Eat this until dinner is ready. It won't be long." She stood and headed for the doorway.

"Ember, I heard you talking to your friend."

She hesitated in the doorway, mentally kicking herself. She'd forgotten about the broken windows. Had she mentioned anything about the officer? She reviewed Bianca's words in her mind, pretending nonchalance. "I'm sorry we woke you. I'll get your food going—"

"I agree with Bianca."

Now he had her attention. "About what?"

"I think you should ask Coste's forgiveness. Maybe he'll take you back."

This conversation had taken a strange turn. "You want me to marry Coste? But—but you're the one who told me about love and waiting for the right man."

He paused. "I did, but—I'm not sure it's wise to wait any longer."

She returned to her chair and sat, her head swimming with confusion. "What are you saying?"

He leaned back against the pillow again, as if gathering his strength. "My little Ember, I want you to be happy. I do. But if you turn down opportunities for happiness so you can care for your sick father, soon there will be no more opportunities left." He coughed and grimaced again.

Ember stood. "I'll get you some water."

"No. Sit."

He wasn't usually this insistent. She lowered herself into her chair again, wincing at the deepness of his cough. It was definitely getting worse. "I'm not pushing away my own happiness. *This* is what I want, to care for you."

When he could breathe again, he watched her with tired eyes. "You're wasting your life waiting for me to recover. I can see it. You wait for me, but I also wait for you."

"I don't understand."

"Death comes for me soon, my Ember."

Ember's heart skipped a beat, and she gripped her chair. "No,

Dai. That's not true. As soon as the medicine arrives, you'll start to feel better again."

"The medicine just postpones what is coming. There have been times I felt death creeping along my bones and shooed it away, telling it my daughter is not ready yet. I want to attend your wedding, to see you happy and settled and cared for the way I can't care for you. But I can't fight it much longer."

The lump in Ember's throat lodged there so tightly she couldn't speak. She shook her head and forced her voice to work. "You don't know that."

"I do, my Ember. Use your gift. It will tell you the truth."

Odd. He'd never been willing to discuss her gift before, much less insisted what she saw was the truth. But it wasn't the truth, not after what she'd seen today with that man Stefan. Her visions had to be possibilities. Nothing more.

"You don't know," she said again. "Nobody does. The stars give me wisps of hope and magic and beautiful things, not death. The medicine will work. I'll increase the dosage when the new bottle comes, and everything will be fine. You just need to trust me."

He studied her face so intensely she shifted in her chair.

"What is it?" she finally asked.

He shook his head as if dismissing a thought. "You've grown strong and determined, as I always hoped. But sometimes your strength blinds you to the reality of our life here. Perhaps it's time for me to arrange a match for you."

"An arranged marriage?" she asked, getting angry. First Bianca had turned against her, and now her father. "I will marry eventually. I swear it. But it will be to a man I choose."

He accepted her words with a long sigh. "I can't bear the thought of you being alone."

"I'm always alone."

Most women were raised with large families and married into even larger families. Noise and chatter were a regular part of Roma life. But for Ember, even a day at the market had its solitude. If her status as Dai's daughter hadn't cast a shadow on her already, her refusal of perfectly good marriages had. And the incident with the chief's son on that terrible night—well, that had clinched it.

He coughed again. "You know what I mean. I hear the children curse you in the streets. I know what their parents are saying. An unattached Roma woman will always be looked upon with suspicion. Without me here as protection, they will find a way to be rid of you. You'll be too vulnerable."

"To what? If you mean Chief Talpa will give me up for homage, he can't. That practice is illegal now."

"It happened to Harman a few years ago."

"They took the man because he was wanted for a crime."

"No," he said firmly. "That's why we allowed it."

She gritted her teeth, barely hiding her frustration. He acted as if she were a ten-year-old child. She'd cared for him for months, and now he wanted to repay her by forcing her into a marriage she'd made it clear she didn't want.

Ember stood and strode toward the doorway. "Let's not talk about this anymore. Nothing will happen to you. Just rest so you can recover and go back to work. I promise we'll have this discussion again then. All right?"

"The stars are never wrong, my light." His voice had gone quiet, and she knew he'd be asleep again soon. "It's time to stop dwelling on what was and prepare for what lies ahead."

# 4

Four hours later, Ember draped the last damp shirt over the line and pinned it into place. She took a small step backward and accidentally clipped a hen, who began squawking in indignation.

She glowered at the bird. "Well, if you'd give me some space to walk, you'd be fine."

Sala the hen eyed her, fluffing its feathers in reply.

"Be careful. I'm hungry, you know."

Sala continued to stare for a moment, then lost interest and walked away.

Their enclosed outdoor living space was larger than most. At forty square yards, the courtyard had plenty of room to complete her chores. But sometimes she resented the open air for the tantalizing scents it carried. Tonight it was her neighbor's Russian tea. She breathed in deeply. It had been so long. Too much had changed in the past few months. Earlier mornings, later nights, more pressure, more chores. Less time to think.

The laundry load had been reduced by half with her father bedridden, but that gave her no comfort. He'd once worn a constant, white-toothed smile that brightened just for her. Now he'd been reduced to a twisted, pained old man. She missed seeing her father's jacket slung across the chair when he came home from the woodshop covered in a light film of sawdust. His excitement at having finished a new piece of furniture, his child-like begging for her to come see. The way he knelt beneath it, bending and pointing to a tiny detail that nobody would ever notice. He believed each piece of furniture better than the last—more intricate, more finely made.

Ember never saw his work the way he did, but his pride made her smile all the same. His last piece was the table in their main room. Her mother had refused to let him sell it, and when she died . . .

Ember cut the thought short and went to empty the water tubs. One for her washing, one for his. She and her father had a cautiously comfortable relationship now, three years after her mother's death. But at first it had been strained. Almost like he blamed her.

He was right to. There was nobody else to blame.

A distant voice floated through the air from the road. She couldn't make out the words for a long while. Finally she recognized the voice as the neighbor's twelve-year-old son's. Was school over for the day already?

"The shuttle is still here," he belted out to his companion. "I saw it, big flag and everything."

Another voice responded, although she couldn't distinguish the words. Their footsteps in the dirt street were loud now.

Her stomach did a little flip, but she ignored the nervousness. Ember had made her decision. Meeting the officer was too much of a risk. She'd sneak out to meet Ambrose for Dai's medicine and then hurry back. Even if the officer made good on his threat to come find her, she'd say she forgot and apologize profusely from the safety of her home.

"Look, there's the old maid's house," the neighbor boy said.

"Should we throw rocks at it?" His younger sister's voice. Jaelle, if Ember remembered correctly. She was about six.

A pause. "Nah. She's probably not there anyway. Market day, remember? The big shuttle? I'm telling you, your ears are stuffed with mud. You never listen to a thing I say."

"Maybe if you'd stop talking once in a while, I'd start listening."

The voices died off, and Ember breathed a sigh of relief. Kids often threw rocks at her house, but whenever she confronted them, they pretended it was an accident. She'd even reported it to their chief, Talpa, who did exactly what he always did. Nothing.

Dai was right about the village hating her, and Bianca was right about the gossip. But it wasn't enough to persuade her. Coste was nice enough, but he'd barely spoken two words to her in his life when he'd proposed. He was nearly twenty years older and a widower. And Babik had only proposed after discovering how much Ember made future-telling on a particularly good day.

Her village was the last kumpania on Earth. The others had been integrated into gadje society and now lived across the galaxy. Only the traditional Roma had been left behind—which meant her prospects were limited.

She didn't want to marry to please her neighbors or Bianca or even Dai. She wanted so much more than an arrangement with someone suitable. She wanted—well, what she'd seen in the vision with Stefan. Just not with *him*, of course.

Ember gave the hanging laundry one last look. It would take longer to dry in the evening, and there was a chance of her clothes being stolen. She'd check on it again after dark.

She emptied the tubs, then went inside and scooped up the plate with Dai's dinner on it—two slices of cooling bread with Bianca's fig jam and the ewe, still perfectly seasoned. She paused near her father's doorway. Should she wake him? Their conversation had taken much out of him, and he spent the day sleeping. Perhaps it was better to let him rest peacefully a bit longer.

The walls took on an orange hue, which meant it was sunset. The officer would be waiting for her now. Was he pacing her market stall, looking at the hill where her village sat? How long would he wait before leaving—or deciding to come find her?

*Let him come. I'm not leaving my father alone so long tonight.*

Her stomach rumbled at the smell of the food beneath her nose. She set the tray down on the table and grabbed a tomato for her own dinner from the box on the counter. She'd give Dai a few more minutes to sleep. In the meantime, she'd take this opportunity to get some long-neglected chores done. It had been far too long since she cleaned, and it would take her mind off that terrible officer.

The shelf caught her eye. A thin layer of dust had settled upon its contents, making each object look a uniform, ashen gray. Her mother's things. Three years later, everything remained just as she'd left it. Dai and Ember had never discussed leaving them out. They just had.

They weren't valuable objects. They'd sold anything of value long ago. No, these objects held memories more than price. Her mother's bridal photo. Ember's first skirt. An old, worn set of tarot cards, the top one askew—her mother's first set of cards, a cheap deck from an old store. A hand mirror. A stained-glass frame with a photograph of their family inside, taken when Ember was fourteen.

Ember carefully picked up the frame and wiped the dust off with a rag, cradling the smooth object in her hands with all the care she could muster. The image had faded slightly in past years, but it was still clear enough to see her parents standing on either side of a younger Ember. Even at fourteen Ember's head had towered over her mother's, though she still wasn't as tall as her father. The women looked somber, not daring to show their teeth, and her father—well, he grinned as if it were the happiest day of his life. It may have been. The traveling photographer was an old friend of Dai's, one he hadn't seen since the military. He'd invited the man to stay with them that night. They'd talked for hours over stew, and the next day the man had presented them with this image before hurrying back to his shuttle.

Ember's hand tightened on the glass. She didn't deserve to handle her mother's beautiful things. Not when it was Ember who had taken her away from all this. The stars knew she hadn't mean to do it, and she still didn't know how she had. She just knew what was.

Her finger caught something sticking out the back. Frowning, she turned it around. A piece of white was caught in the small hatch. She pulled it open and caught the object as it came fluttering out and landed in her lap. Another photograph?

Ember secured the hatch again and gently set the frame on the shelf. Then she picked up the paper with trembling hands and examined it. It was an article. The paper was thin and brittle against her fingertips, as if printed from a machine, like in the old days. A much younger version of Dai smiled faintly from the photograph. He was perhaps her age, maybe younger, and wore a dark uniform with several pins dotting the collar, although the uniform was slightly different than the one the officer had worn today. It looked more like a jacket. He held a large rectangular piece of glass with tiny words etched into it. A string of thick black words was printed across the top, just above his head: "Lucinello Wins Intergalactic Service Award."

Under the image was a bit of text in Common. Ember strained to read the strange words.

*Mario Nicholas Lucinello, a product of the Empire's successful flicker breeding program, was awarded the Intergalactic Military Service Award Friday night for exceptional performance in last week's battle at Germini Minefield. In a rare speech after the award was presented, the emperor himself praised Lucinello, calling him "a priceless trophy for all those who doubt the Empire's pledge of protection for systems within the Empire." Lucinello declined to speak upon receiving the award, indicating that he was overcome with gratitude at the cabinet's generosity. General Kane also spoke but would not elaborate on the military hero's next assignment. "We're taking him all the way to the top," Kane told reporters before the event concluded. While the meaning of the statement is unclear, many experts agree Empyrean is a strong possibility. If true, at age nineteen, Lucinello will be the youngest flicker in history to be allowed access to Empyrean. Some strategists speculate that Lucinello's next assignments will include combat in the Archaean System—*

The text ended there, torn off midsentence. Ember read the paper several times and then let it drop to the floor. *Mario Nicholas Lucinello.* The village knew him as Nicholae, and that was what her mother had called him. Nobody had ever questioned it. Who'd saved this clipping, and why? Perhaps Dai was proud of his accomplishments and wanted to remember his glory days in secret.

But that felt wrong. He had never acted proud of his time in the military. Maybe something had happened between the article's publication and his arrival on Earth.

She had so many questions now. What was a flicker? What did it mean that he was the product of a breeding program? And where was Empyrean? She'd never heard of that planet before.

Ember sat there for a long time, absorbing the words. But the questions overwhelmed her, and it soon grew dark as the sun disappeared for the night. Surely the officer knew she wasn't coming by now. Hopefully he was already gone.

She picked up her father's food and entered his room, determined to wake him and demand answers. But he looked so peaceful and still, his breathing finally regular. She couldn't do it.

She set his plate on the chair next to his bed where he would see it upon awakening. Then she flipped on the lantern in the corner to its lowest setting. As she left, she gave him one last look.

"The medicine will work," she whispered. "You will get better, and we'll move on together because I refuse to lose you, too."

# 5

She waited until the village went quiet, then snuck out to the hollow where she always met Ambrose. He wasn't there. She waited nearly two hours, until the air went chill and her teeth chattered, before going home. Eight nights she'd tried to meet him. What could possibly be holding him up? Didn't he understand how desperate their situation was?

Her dreams that night were jumbled, peppered with space battles and hard-faced officers demanding their futures told. Each time she declined, they shot her and she crumpled to the floor, reaching out for Dai. But he was already dead, his body just out of reach.

"Please," she found herself begging. "Let me help him."

But every time she stood up, the men raised their weapons and insisted she read their futures.

She finally sat up in bed and looked around but saw only darkness. Her father's breathing, slow and regular, sounded from the next room over. Just a nightmare.

As she was beginning to roll over again, she heard something—a scraping from outside her room, barely distinguishable above her father's breathing.

Ember strained to hear it again, but there was nothing except the gentle clucking of the hens in the courtyard. Whatever this sound was, it was inside the house.

*Sala probably got inside again,* she assured herself. The hen was constantly hopping through their other window, low as it was and without glass. Best to return her to the courtyard before they woke Dai.

Something scraped again.

This time it sounded remarkably heavy. A boot, perhaps.

Panic rose within her, and adrenaline shot through her system as fear got the better of her. She was paralyzed, unable to move. It was too much like the night everything had gone wrong. The memory leaped back into her mind before she could block it.

*Ember's eyes flew open as a hand clamped over her mouth and nose. She gasped for air but got a terrible gritty taste instead. The smell of dirt overwhelmed her, filling her lungs, and she coughed and thrashed her arms about until the hand tore away. The two dark figures on either side of her bed scrambled to secure her.*

*Babik cursed softly in the darkness. "Hold her still already. There are two of you and one of her." It was the chief's son, the man whose offer of marriage she had rejected the day before.*

*"You hold her down, then," someone else whispered. "Get your own teeth kicked in."*

*She tried to scream as she thrashed, but a hand clamped over her mouth again before she could get a sound out.*

*Babik swore again. "There's not enough rope."*

*"Well, I'm not waiting an hour for you to get more," the second man hissed. "Just claim her now, before someone comes."*

The scraping sound was closer now, coming every few seconds.

Ember swallowed back the fear and slid off her bed, landing in a crouch. Surprise was the only weapon she had, and she intended to use it.

Well, there was one other weapon, but she would never use it again.

The intruder paused for a moment, then brushed through the divider cloth, breathing heavily, shakily, sounding almost afraid.

The dark figure made its way to the bed and slowly lowered an arm. There was something small and dark in the hand extended toward her.

Ember didn't want to know what it was. She scrambled to her feet and bolted through the divider as the intruder gave a soft cry of surprise. She recognized the voice. Babik.

He was married now with a child on the way, but apparently that hadn't stopped him from wanting to finish what he had started.

She raced for her father's doorway, but a large figure moved to block her and she slammed into the man before she could stop, his arms enveloping her, crushing her until she could barely breathe.

"Running instead of fighting tonight?" the deep voice asked. Talpa, the chief and Babik's father. It seemed he had decided to accompany his son this time. The man's breath smelled heavily of alcohol. She bolted to the side, but he grabbed her hair and spun her backward against him, then wrapped one massive arm around her throat.

She tried to cry out, but the pressure on her windpipe increased even more until she thought it would fold right in half. Her head began to spin.

Talpa took several wide steps toward the front door, pulling her alongside him, like a child dragging a teddy bear.

*Not enough air.*

She fought and kicked and tried to turn her head, but the

harder she fought, the tighter Talpa's grip became. Blackness had begun to close in by the time they stepped outside, but the sharp coolness of the night air blasted her back to consciousness.

Rough hands fumbled with her wrists, but Talpa's grip didn't loosen.

"Tighter than that," Talpa hissed, and a sharp pain sliced through her wrists. Only then did Talpa release her. She crumpled to her knees, gasping and sucking in precious oxygen.

Next to the Roma chief stood a man in black, surrounded by four guards. One guard was taller than the rest, but she couldn't see their faces in the darkness.

"Is that sufficient, High Commander?" Talpa asked.

The man motioned to the taller guard, who raised a hand lantern to Ember's eyes. Ember squinted against the painful brightness.

"That's her, sir," a female guard confirmed in a strangely deep voice.

"Very well," the officer said. "I will make a note of your village's homage in our records. But I will not be so kind when I return if you have neglected to pay what is due yet again."

"Of course, High Commander," Talpa said. "As you say. Whatever you'd like is my pleasure."

The officer gave Babik a disdainful look. "You might consider sending your boys into the military rather than marrying them off young. Then your people might actually be worth something to the emperor."

"I will . . . consider that, Commander."

"Think long and hard." The man turned to Ember. "I warned you to come as ordered, gypsy girl. Now we're out of time for testing. To the ship."

Ember, whose breaths came short and fast now, pushed to her feet and began to stumble toward the front door.

The tall guard whipped out her weapon with surprising

speed. There was no sound, but an unbelievably strong force slammed into Ember's chest. A scream ripped from her throat.

Then there was darkness.

# 6

Ember's throat burned.

She forced her eyes open and lifted her head, her kinked neck protesting the sudden movement. She struggled to rub it but couldn't move her arms. They were secured to the armrests of her chair.

Not a chair. A seat.

Ember took in the vibration of the floor at her feet, the hum of an engine outside. The windows spaced evenly apart. The dark figures draped in their seats around her. Someone was snoring.

She swung her head to peer out the window but saw only darkness and the faint golden glow of a thruster. The cabin, too, was dark except for the illuminated lines indicating an aisle to her left.

An aisle. Windows. Seats. *A shuttle.*

Her breaths came too fast now. The air circulating around her was stale and cold, and it made the deep pain in her throat worse. She tried to thrash around, but the bonds around her arms bit painfully into her skin. Her upper body and stomach were secured by a harness. She tried to raise her feet, but they were completely numb.

*No, no, no. This can't be real.*

"Hold on," a voice said from across the aisle. The man unlatched his harness and approached her. It was too dark to see his face, but his voice was familiar somehow. He knelt and fumbled with the bonds at her feet, and the tightness eased immediately. He rose and sat on the empty seat beside her. "Is that better?"

Ember recognized him now—that man from the market yesterday, the one whose future she'd read. Stefan. She was definitely on the Empire ship.

She looked around. Several more rows of seats lined the cabin, and by the sounds of breathing, they were all occupied. "I shouldn't be here." She swung her legs up. They felt disconnected somehow. It would take awhile for the blood to flow correctly again. "Why am I here? How dare you tie me up like this."

He put up a hand. "Whoa, there, future-teller. I had nothing to do with it. And keep your voice down, all right? Everyone's asleep, and you don't want this group mad at you. They've been staring at you all day, trying to figure out why Commander Kane ordered us to swing so far out of our way to get you."

She choked. "All day?"

"You've been out almost twenty-four hours. The guards must have used a high-level stunner." He sat back with a grunt, as if he didn't approve.

Stunners. *Guards.* The memory slammed into her consciousness all at once, suddenly overwhelming her.

The officer and his guards. Talpa and his son betraying her. No—worse than that.

The chief had *sold* her as homage to the Empire.

She gave a strangled cry. Her father would have woken to an empty house, wondering where she was. He couldn't get out of bed to prepare his food. And what about his medicine?

"I have to go home," she hissed. "You have to tell them. If we turn around right now—"

"Shh," Stefan whispered. "In the morning they'll send someone to talk to you, to explain everything."

She stared at him. "I don't want them to *explain*. I want to go home. My father is sick—he needs me."

"I already know that."

"What is that supposed to mean?"

He paused, looking sheepish. "Most people have a natural shield, but it's thinnest when you're asleep. It makes it really easy for a flicker to break in." He took a deep breath and went on in a rush. "I wasn't looking, exactly. It's just that most of us have practiced enough that we're protected when we sleep. Yours was wide open. I swear I didn't look very far. I just wanted to see what happened. After the reading, I mean."

Ember stared at him. *Wide open?* See what happened? What was he talking about?

*Flicker.* The word was barely familiar, almost like a wisp of memory. She tried to remember where she'd heard it, then decided it didn't matter. The only thing of importance was getting home.

Someone across the room mumbled in their sleep. It was a girl, her chin resting forward on her chest. It didn't look very comfortable.

"Don't worry," Stefan continued. "I don't think anyone else cared enough to probe you. But you'll want to train in mental defenses as soon as we get to Avegard Station."

She rested her head against the back of the seat, suddenly weary. The circulation was flowing in her feet now, sending pain all the way to her toes. "Don't *worry*?" She gritted her teeth. "No, no. This is not okay. Tell your commander I want to talk to him right now."

He chuckled. "You don't make demands of a high commander, particularly Kane. It's an honor just to be on the same ship."

Commander Kane. *Flicker.* Of course—she'd read about it in the article hidden behind her family's photograph. Something about her father winning an award and Kane saying he would take him to the top. And a sentence about a flicker breeding program.

But what did that have to do with her?

"What is a flicker?" she asked cautiously.

He watched her for a long moment. "You're serious, aren't you?"

"Will you shut up?" someone whined from across the cabin. "Some of us are trying to sleep here."

Stefan lowered his voice to a whisper. "A flicker can see things others can't."

Ember's mother had trained her well in future-telling. She'd described it as a combination of card reading and people reading. But it had never been that way for Ember. To her, the ability was examining light, almost like sifting through memories. Visions, flashes of possibilities given her from the stars. "How does it work?"

"You already know. You gave quite the demonstration yesterday."

She studied her hands. "Tell me anyway."

He shrugged. "It manifests a little differently for everyone, but one thing is always the same. Each living being has an inner light, something religions call a spirit, or soul. Even scientists had to admit there was a part of a person that could be sensed but not seen. You know, that feeling of being watched, or a sense of dread when there's danger. Some say a person's light merges with their own consciousness as their soul passes on. That's why the dying see their life pass before their eyes."

*Inner light.* That was what she called it too. His words settled in her heart, sending a chill down her body. His description was exactly right. "Go on."

"Scientists have tried for centuries, but they couldn't re-create that light in machines or AI or anything else. It was a mystery—until the first flickers were born. They described the soul as a flickering light, something that held a person's past and future, like DNA. I guess the name stuck." He grinned, the shadows from the window crossing his face in a series of dark lines. "Now we're the rarest, most sought-after beings in the universe."

Anger flared up inside. He made it sound like such a pleasure to be here. She wasn't a piece of gold to be mined, by Kane or anyone else. "And this ship is headed where?"

"Flicker testing. They didn't tell you?"

"No," she growled.

He grunted again and muttered something under his breath.

It had never occurred to her that there were others like her out there. Connecting with a person's light to see their future was a beautiful gift, but she hadn't considered the ramifications on a larger scale. This type of power in the Empire's hands was a scary thing to contemplate.

"By the way," Stefan continued, "I noticed that you closed your eyes when you read my future yesterday. You'll want to get over that habit. It leaves you vulnerable to attack."

*Attack*? Who would want to attack her? She wasn't dangerous . . . was she? There it was again, that deep-rooted discomfort telling her something was very wrong. Whatever training they intended for her, she wanted no part of it.

"My father is ill," she whispered. "I can't leave him for training or anything else. You have to help me get home."

He was quiet for a long moment. All she could hear was snoring and the low hum of the engines outside. "They shouldn't have done this to you. It wasn't right. And to think that I had a hand in it, however unintentional. I'm really sorry."

It was a long, roundabout way of saying he couldn't help her. Ember gritted her teeth. If only she'd been more careful. She should have known better than to tell a man's future in front of an officer. There was only one thing going for her. Kane suspected she was a flicker, but he didn't know for sure yet. That meant she could still convince him otherwise. "When do we arrive?"

"In the morning." He leaned around the cabin. "Speaking of which, I should probably catch some sleep. Unlike certain people on this ship, I didn't get to sleep the day through."

"One last thing."

"What's that?"

"How much did you see of my memories?"

It took him a second to understand. "Oh, not much. You at a funeral. Your mom's, I think. And your friend's wedding. Really, all I wanted to know was how you were kidnapped. I swear I didn't look deeper than that."

She couldn't read his face in this light. If he was lying, he hid it well. "Then promise me you'll never, ever go poking around inside my mind without my permission again."

Stefan grinned. "You have my word." He stood and stepped over her, then returned to his seat across the aisle.

They'd reach a station in the morning. If she fooled Kane into thinking she wasn't a flicker, she could be home in two days. Maybe it wouldn't be too late.

*Stars,* she breathed, *keep Dai safe until I return. Please.*

She reached out into the wide expanse of space, searching for a single flickering light across the galaxy. He was too far away, of course. She knew that.

But she didn't stop reaching, continuing her search for hours, straining until sleep stole her once again.

# 7

Ember was stunned as she stood in the doorway upon their arrival. When Stefan had called their destination Avegard Station, Ember had pictured an oversized spaceship. But the city that spread before her was far beyond anything she could have imagined. If this was a station, it had to be the largest one in the universe.

The huge white city spanned as far as she could see, its buildings rising like mountains. Colorful laser ads appeared in the atmosphere overhead, spewing messages about body shaping technology and some entertainment competition. A dull hum rose from the city's streets as its citizens moved about. The city seemed lit from above, although Ember couldn't see a single source of light. It had to be artificial.

She took a deep breath, expecting fresh air like she was used to, but all that filled her lungs was the same stale air as on the ship. It made sense. This was a station, after all.

Stefan came up beside her, seeming pleased at her reaction. "It's an entire planet. They keep the ships beneath the surface for protection."

Ember frowned. "They protect the ships but leave the people exposed?"

He laughed. "You have a lot to learn about the Empire."

That irritating girl, Eris, appeared at his side. She slid herself between Ember and Stefan, stretching her arms. "It feels so good to walk around. What a dreadful trip. And a whole four days longer than it should have been." She didn't glare at Ember, but her point was clear.

Ember moved aside so the other passengers could get by. Her legs were stiff, and the welts from her two-day-old bonds itched, as they'd only been removed this morning. As beautiful as the city was, stepping outside the ship felt like a betrayal. She wished she could march to the cockpit and demand the pilot take her straight home, but the cockpit door was locked. She'd already tested it.

A girl with four knotted ponytails hesitated at the hatch beside Ember, covering her mouth and nose with both hands. She waited a full five seconds before stepping out, then finally took a deep, gasping breath. Freckles flooded her face and arms.

"Are you all right?" Ember asked, confused at the performance.

"Fine. Just testing the air." She thrust her hand out. "I'm Mariana. My friends call me Mar because I love the ocean. You're from a water planet, so you get it, right? My people sent me even though I didn't want to come."

Ember returned the handshake and pulled away a second early. She missed everything, not just the ocean. Her village, Dai, Bianca, familiar food. The ship had supplied food packets, but they just weren't the same. And the light here felt so unnatural. The only piece of home she still owned were her skirt and blouse, and that was only because she'd fallen onto her bed before undressing two nights before. Stars, she was grateful for that now.

"Well, you coming? Mar asked. "I mean, I'd rather avoid

orientation too, but you can't stay on the ship. They're going to send it below, and the pressurization would kill you."

"I—I'm coming." Ember stepped off the ship, still gazing at the city before them. The ramp turned sharply into another white building with metal accents. The ship's crew had already begun to clean the passenger area behind her. Had Commander Kane already exited? Where were the guards?

Mar walked down the ramp without looking back. "I've only been here once, when I was too young to remember. I heard they originally painted the buildings white to keep them from getting too hot. It used to be a lot closer to the second sun, you know. The artificial atmosphere could only do so much." She shrugged. "But then the sun's flares kept messing with their tech, so they moved the station back. I guess they decided to keep the white."

"They moved it," Ember murmured, jogging to keep up with Mar. "Just like that." She kept glancing to the side of the ramp, but it was too steep a drop to jump down. No wonder the guards hadn't felt it necessary to follow her. There was nowhere for her to go but inside.

"I've heard the shopping is great too," Mar continued. "They have *everything* here. We'll have to go sometime. If they ever let us out, that is."

Shopping. Maybe they had her father's medicine here. If she found enough of it, she could bring home a year's worth. Maybe even two. That had to be long enough to get him better.

*Focus.* Ember didn't have time to shop for medicine or anything else. Her first priority was to convince them she didn't belong here. If necessary, she would make it clear she didn't intend to cooperate so they'd *have* to send her home. And if that didn't work, she'd find a way to escape.

Mar went on ahead, chattering about another station she'd visited once. Ember sighed and followed the line of excited recruits—flickers—down the ramp and into the building looming above her.

~

The corridor inside was white like the outside, with a tall, looming ceiling that left Ember feeling uncomfortable and overexposed.

An unnaturally tall woman in a black uniform met them inside, and Ember immediately recognized her as one of Kane's guards. Now that Kane wasn't here to command her attention, Ember took a long look at the woman. Her pink hair was chin length and streaked with black. And her uniform's trousers fit much too snugly around her rear end.

"Call me Talon," the woman said in that low voice of hers. "You will follow me." She turned and walked briskly down the hall, her long strides eating up the ground like a giraffe's. The crowd of young people followed, some trotting to keep up.

They reached the end of a hallway and found themselves in front of a single door.

"File inside quietly for uniform assignment," Talon said. "Men to the left, women to the right. Anything else, choose a side. You will wear your official uniform from this moment on, for everyone's safety. Those caught wearing anything else outside their quarters will be severely punished."

She looked at the door, and it slid open as if on command. The crowd pushed forward, each flicker determined to be among the first to get their uniform.

Ember hung back, fingering her skirt. This wasn't good.

"Go on," Talon said, motioning to the doorway. "Or shall I tell the high commander you've decided not to cooperate? I'm sure he can find you a nice, comfy cell."

Ending up in a prison cell would make getting home to Dai very hard. Ember swallowed and went through the door. Talon followed, and the door immediately shut after her. Automatic doors. She'd heard of such things even in Earth's history, but seeing them work was disturbing. How did the door know when to close?

She followed the group to the right. When she reached the front, a woman with braided hair greeted her. Finally a hairstyle she recognized. Her tag read *Sindi.*

"Medium," the woman said to herself, looking Ember up and down. "May be small in the waist, but you're tall enough that you'll need the length. Here." She retrieved a black bundle from the table behind her. "Put these on."

Ember took the bundle and separated the pieces. Maybe it wouldn't be so bad. She didn't like the color black, but if the fabric was appropriate . . .

She held the trousers up and groaned. "They call this a uniform?"

Sindi turned back to her. "They're formfitting, but you'd be surprised how soft the fabric is. Very forgiving." Her nose wrinkled as she eyed Ember's long skirt.

Ember snorted. "I'm not wearing that."

Sindi held up the black trousers and examined them. "No holes, no signs of wear. I think you'll have to explain to me where this aversion is coming from. We could try a large, but it would fall right off those tiny hips of yours."

"I don't—I've never—"

The woman's eyes went wide, and she dropped the trousers back onto the table. "You've never worn trousers before."

Ember nodded, relieved that the woman understood.

It began as a long, sharp cough. Sindi's shoulders shook with the power of it. Then Ember realized the woman was laughing.

"Talon," she called out through bursts of sound. "Some assistance, please."

The lanky, pink-haired guard peeked her head through the divider. "Problem?" Ember cringed, even though she was still fully clothed and it was a woman.

"This girl says she's never worn trousers before. She wants to keep her skirt."

"She refuses her uniform?"

"I think you could say that, yes."

Talon glared at Ember. "Put on the uniform, or I'll drag you into the open and dress you myself. The choice is yours."

Ember scowled. Nobody would dress her, especially in public. But wearing that . . . that . . . *thing* was absolutely indecent. "I'm not staying. I'm going home soon."

Talon shrugged. "Makes no difference to me." She shoved the curtain aside and began to approach.

Ember growled and snatched the trousers from Sindi's grasp, glowering at the guard with all her might. Now both Talon and Sindi were laughing.

"The jacket, too," Sindi said, holding another bundle of black fabric.

Ember changed quickly, her face warming as the two women watched.

The room was nearly empty by the time she emerged from behind the curtain. Feeling utterly exposed in her new trousers, Ember rubbed her thighs uncomfortably. The fabric was thin, closer to long underwear than anything. Sindi had disappeared, and all Ember could hear was soft whispering from across the room.

A long mirror covered the wall facing her. Ember had seen mirrors plenty of times—her mother had owned one—but never this big. She'd never actually seen her entire body in a mirror before. She almost didn't dare look, wearing this dreadful outfit that left so little to the imagination. But she couldn't resist a peek.

In the mirror, a woman with black, flowing hair glowered back at her. The pants hugged her lower body so tightly that pink spread to her cheeks. It gave her face an angry glow. She didn't look Roma at all.

"Are you sure the women here don't wear anything over this?" Ember muttered.

"One more thing," Sindi said, appearing from nowhere. "Records say you're from one of the outer planets, so I'm required to give you this. Combats the air change and makes sure you don't spread anything." She grabbed Ember's arm, pulled up the sleeve, and stabbed her with something tiny and sharp.

Ember shrieked and scrambled back, but the pain subsided instantly. She stared at her arm. Only the tiniest speck of blood was visible. "What was that?"

The woman put the device into a bag and dropped it into a bin against the wall. "Just an immunization, dear. You don't have those on Earth either?" That set the woman off in her laughter again.

Ember chose to make her way quickly out of the room rather than argue. It wasn't until the door whooshed closed behind her that she remembered she'd left her skirt and blouse behind.

She ran back to the door, but it didn't open. She pounded on it without success, then tried pushing it open. It wouldn't budge.

"This is the third time you've made trouble in twenty minutes," Talon said, walking up behind her in the narrow corridor. "Is this what we should expect during your stay?"

Ember had to crane her neck to meet the woman's gaze. "My belongings," Ember said. "I left them inside."

Talon waved a long-fingered hand. "In the incinerator already, I'm sure. They burn everything right away." She eyed Ember's hair and frowned. "Particularly when there's a question of sanitation."

Her skirt and blouse she could replace. But her mother's hand-painted tarot cards in the hidden pocket were priceless. Now they were gone forever, just like the woman who had given them to her.

"None of the others brought luggage either, gypsy girl," Talon said. “You don’t see them crying about it. They’re all seated, waiting for orientation like you’re supposed to be.”

“None of them were kidnapped, then,” Ember snapped. “So much for my rights as an Empire citizen. I don’t care what abilities you think I have. I don’t belong here and I’m going home.”

Talon’s eyes narrowed. A chill settled over Ember as she remembered what this woman was capable of. Her abduction had happened quickly, but she was certain Talon was the one who’d cut her down with the stunner. At the moment, the woman looked as if she longed to do it again.

Talon’s voice went low and dangerous. “You have no idea what you’re dealing with, gypsy. You *belong* where High Commander Kane wants you. Every one of this year’s batch has been marked since they tested positive around age five or six. They’ve been preparing for testing week ever since. You somehow escaped the Empire’s notice—”

“Marked?” Ember interrupted. “You mean branded. Like livestock.”

Talon was silent for a long moment, her long fingers hovering over the stunner at her belt. Ember knew she had crossed a line, but she forced herself to meet the tall woman’s gaze.

“Interrupt me again,” the woman whispered, “and I will render you unable to travel anywhere, Earth or otherwise. Now go. Orientation is about to begin.”

# 8

The building felt so modern, so ship-like, that she had nearly forgotten she was standing on a giant white planet station, but when she stepped into the briefing room, it was impossible to forget. The room was shaped like a glass dome and had a clear ceiling exposed to the "sky" above. But it wasn't like an earthly sky—stormy or clear or sunny. It was a murky gray. No clouds, no stars. Something drab and in-between. She wasn't sure why they'd even bothered with this glass dome if there was nothing to see above it.

Most of the flickers were already seated. Ember caught a glimpse of Stefan near the front next to Eris. She muttered something, and he chuckled. Ember instinctively gripped where her skirt had once been, but in its place was a smooth, soft fabric that hugged her curves.

Feeling as if the entire room was watching her, she scanned the neat rows for an empty seat. Mar waved to her from the back and motioned to a chair. Relieved, Ember headed toward her just as Talon entered. The woman made it to the podium in four strides and began to speak.

"Today is an important day for you, flickers, one we look

forward to every year." Her deep voice was amplified by speakers in the walls, but Ember couldn't see a microphone. Their tech was so strange.

"There are seventy-three of you here, from forty-one sectors. Many of you have trained for testing week since childhood. Many of you probably thought your twentieth year would never come. Others, however, are woefully unprepared for what is ahead." She didn't glance at Ember, but several flickers did. Ember kept her face impassive. She was nineteen, not twenty, but she doubted that was enough reason to send her home.

"You have a remarkable gift, one that makes you incredibly valuable to the emperor. That's why you'll spend your week in comfort, housed in some of our finest rooms and eating the very best food. Each of you is a powerful weapon in our battle against the enemy. Unfortunately, not every flicker is right for our program. Either you have what we need, or you don't."

The silence was stifling. The air squeezed around Ember so tightly she could almost feel Talpa's bone-breaking arm around her throat again. One word reverberated in her mind, overtaking her thoughts until she couldn't see anything else. *Weapon.*

It was exactly like her father's article. They were making flickers into weapons.

Talon raised her voice again. "Your testing will consist of three phases over three days. The first begins tomorrow morning at 08:00. You will receive the room number on your wristbands. And, no, I'm not authorized to reveal what the first phase entails, so don't ask." She pressed her lips together in a grimace that was probably supposed to be a smile. A few people chuckled uncomfortably.

Ember barely heard. Weapon. Battle. Enemy. *Closing your eyes leaves you exposed,* Stefan had said. What kind of twisted system was this? Reading a person's inner light was an intimate experience, a gift from the stars. Was the Empire training a force of readers to spy on their enemies? Or was there something even darker going on here?

"The room number to your quarters will appear on your wristband soon," Talon continued. "You have the afternoon to explore the city. When your wristband begins to vibrate, return to the station immediately and report to the cafeteria by 1700. Stragglers will be disqualified."

The room began to fill with excited whispers. Talon stepped down from the platform and exited, although the guards lining the walls stayed.

Mar leaned over. "They're testing us already. They'll track us around the city."

Blood pulsed in Ember's ears. The room seemed to be closing in on her. Ember had danced along the edges of what was moral by profiting from her gift, but using it to win a war? This was absolutely and completely wrong. She couldn't stay in this terrible place a moment longer.

The flicker recruits stood and headed for the double doors at the rear. A group of several men and one woman joined Stefan and Eris, apparently discussing where they would go. Ember brushed past them. The doors slid open for her, allowing her outside.

The city reflected painfully against her eyes. She missed the casual chaos of Earth, the colors and textures and familiar ground. There wasn't a sign of dirt anywhere. Occasionally plants broke up the whiteness, but they were obviously fake. Some were even bright colors, like purple and orange.

"Gypsy girl!" Mar pulled up beside her, breathing hard. "How could you go barging off without me?"

"Roma," Ember corrected. "And I'm Gheorghe Ember of the Argyle Beach Kumpania."

"Uh, I'm not going to remember that. You go by what, exactly?"

"Ember."

"Got it. So where to first?"

She looked behind them at the group passing through the doors and laughing. They moved easily, as if they'd been here before. They probably had, if they were some of the lifelong-preparation flickers Talon had mentioned. She spotted Stefan in the center. Eris had her arm through his.

Ember hadn't told him about the kissing vision, thank the stars, and it didn't seem like he'd seen it in her earlier. She would just pretend it never happened and move on.

Ember thought quickly. "To find some medicine." And if she was lucky, find a ship to take her home.

"Oh." Mar frowned and slowed her step. "That doesn't sound very exciting. Don't you want to head for a bar? This is the best tech center in eight sectors. They'll have the best VR stations ever built. I mean, there's this one at the Grande that supposedly uses an antigravity module with—"

"You go ahead, then. Don't let me stop you." Ember continued on her path, following the others down a massive stairway to the city street below.

Mar scowled and caught up to her. "Well, I guess we can run your errand first. I mean, since you don't know your way around."

Mar technically didn't either, but Ember didn't feel like pointing that out.

They made their way down six flights of steps before the street came into view. She felt light-headed for a moment and paused along the wall, allowing people to pass.

"You okay?" Mar asked, pulling up beside her. "I know the air's different here, but they were supposed to give you an adjustment when you got your uniform. I didn't need one, but I totally understand if you're feeling an oxygen percentage discrepancy."

"I'm fine." Ember stepped slowly down to a sidewalk packed with flickers. They seemed to be crowding toward a sky-train platform. She turned the other direction, determined to walk. She'd had enough air travel to last her a lifetime.

Ember headed down the sidewalk, already deep in thought. Would Talpa turn her in when she got home? Would the Empire care enough to look for her again? Was Dai still alive?

*One step at a time,* she reminded herself as Mar fell into step beside her.

~

"It's called Latitude H2C," Ember told the pharmacist for the third time. "La-ti-tude. It comes in small round pills, a brown color."

"I say again," the woman replied. "A hospital drug. Cannot get here."

The pharmacy was a tiny, two-level building with nothing but photographs of smiling people lining the walls. The occasional image displayed blinking words in Common. It seemed the Empire allowed only one language on their stations.

Ember sighed. "Where else should I look?"

Mar groaned from the doorway. This was the fourth pharmacy they'd visited in two hours, and even Ember was beginning to lose hope.

"Cannot get anywhere but hospital." The woman looked impatient. "I must go now." She turned and headed toward the back.

"Come on, Ember," Mar said. "Let's take a break. Remember the Grande, that VR place I told you about? It's only a fifteen-minute walk from here. Maybe we'll find someone there who can help you. Besides, it'll look bad if all we do is visit pharmacies. The Empire's tracking us, remember?"

Ember tried to thank the pharmacist, but she had already disappeared behind a wall. Mar was already striding down the walkway before Ember got there. City trains zoomed past, the wind whipping at Mar's knotted ponytails, but she didn't seem to mind. A bit of her prior excitement had begun to come back.

"Fine," Ember muttered. If Dai's medicine was regulated that strictly, the only way to get it would be the underground. Maybe a bar wasn't such a bad idea.

She had just gone to follow Mar when a female voice hissed, "Hey, flicker girl."

Ember stopped and turned. The pharmacist she'd just spoken with stood in the back entrance, waving at her.

"I think I have what you seek. You wait behind." The woman motioned behind the building and disappeared inside.

Ember searched the crowd for Mar's head and found her half a block up, striding purposefully toward an intersection. She'd catch up to her in a minute.

Ember circled the building until the street was out of sight, then made her way to the back door and waited.

The pharmacist reappeared a moment later and handed Ember a container. "It is this, yes?"

Ember took the container, excitement rising within her. She slid open the top and looked inside, then felt her shoulders sag in relief. "Yes! This is it. Now I just need to ship it to Earth."

The woman's eyes widened. "Oh, no, no. I cannot do for you. Is too expensive."

*Expensive.* Ember had forgotten about that part. She pulled out her wristband and checked her account. Stefan's 200 credits plus another nineteen from the previous week. "What does this cost? I'll give you all I have." She held out her band for the woman to see.

A glimmer of mischief shone in the woman's dark eyes. She didn't even look at the screen. "You are flicker, yes? I know the jacket."

Ember swallowed, everything within her crying out to resist the label. She wore the uniform, but that didn't change who she was. "You want me to read your future?"

"No. You will read my husband." The pharmacist took

Ember's arm and pulled her through the door before she could protest.

The woman took her to a flight of narrow stairs that led above the shop. Ember found her mind whirling at this new development. What did this woman want her to do? Was the man having a secret affair his wife wanted exposed? Was he looking for a job?

They reached a bedroom with a figure covered in several blankets. The room stunk of medications and unwashed fabric. The woman made her way to her husband's side and took his hand.

"You tell me if he lives," she said, her former mischief gone. She was completely somber now. "You tell the truth, I give medicine."

Ember stepped over to the other side of the bed and winced at what she saw. The man looked dead already, his features pale and sunken. Even his chest seemed to cave in strangely. She wasn't sure she wanted to know this man's future.

"Why isn't he in the hospital?" she asked.

"They send him home. You read him now."

"Very well," Ember said with forced enthusiasm. She closed her eyes and began to hum. She felt her own light pulse and extended her reach. The man's light was weak, fluttering. He was very near death.

She reached in and experienced bits and pieces of his past. His childhood on Tantom as the fourth of twenty-eight children. His time at the university when he met his wife, who was training to become a pharmacist. Their eleven children, three of whom were taken in the war. His time serving the Union as a spy.

She straightened, jerking out of that particular memory. The Union. She'd heard of the group before. Was that the enemy Talon had mentioned? Surely the pharmacist didn't know about her husband's true profession, or she would never have asked Ember to read him. She wore the Empire's uniform, after all.

*Don't worry,* she told the man inwardly. *Your secret is safe with me.*

She reached for the light again and saw his pain, deep and raw. She saw herself standing above the man with her eyes closed. She pushed forward, straining to see what lay beyond, but it was a strange blur of color and sound. And then nothing.

Ember swallowed hard and opened her eyes, settling her gaze upon the anxious woman across the bed from her. The pharmacist watched her with wide eyes, then her lips parted slightly in understanding. She lowered her gaze upon her husband.

"I'm sorry," Ember whispered. "There's not much time left."

The wife let out a sob and fell upon her husband's chest with a high-pitched wail. The husband's arm moved slightly as if to comfort her, but there was nothing to be done. Ember had just removed whatever hope remained.

"Go," the woman said between her tears.

Ember held out the container of pills, but the woman shoved it back at her and returned to her wailing.

"I really am sorry," she said again, the woman's sobbing her only reply.

## 9

The vision of that sick man haunted Ember as she wandered the city. She shivered as she remembered his blank expression, his pain. Did the man still live? Was Dai as helpless and limp right now as that man had been?

At least the dying man wasn't alone. She couldn't say the same for her father.

She walked for forty-five minutes and didn't see a single dock or landing pad. She watched the sky above her, hoping to catch sight of a shuttle, a freighter, *anything*. But the skies remained empty. She finally asked a man on the street for directions to a transport station but got a confused stare in return.

"This entire planet's the station," he said. "There's only one authorized landing pad, and that's where you arrived."

Ember sighed. It seemed she'd be heading back to the massive white testing building after all. Maybe if she hurried there would be time to search the building for a way to get home.

She jogged back, winding through the ever-busy streets, suddenly weary of the lights and noise. A guard scanned her wristband at the bottom of the steps before motioning her onward. She climbed the six flights of steps, which seemed to have multiplied since her descent earlier, and made her way inside. Thankfully the corridors were still relatively empty.

For ten minutes she wandered down a series of corridors that all looked identical. Occasionally she passed a soldier in a crisp uniform. They didn't look surprised at the sight of Ember's jacket, but she noticed they gave her a wide berth. What a strange situation for flickers here—being forced to become a weapon for the Empire and being shunned for it at the same time.

She thought about the other flickers, probably returning to this building right now. Were they reading the people they met, forcing their way past the defenses regular citizens weren't even aware of? Were they gathering information to turn in to the Empire and get a pat on the head?

Such knowledge would be dangerous in a place like this, especially for people like the dying man, who had hidden ties to the Union. No wonder flickers were so tightly controlled.

She turned yet another corner and pulled up short. Stefan was striding toward her. He stopped and grinned. "Had enough of the city already?"

She forced a smile. "Just tired. You?"

"I've seen it a few times before. Fifty, eighty maybe." He shrugged. "I grew up on Dalimane Station, and we visited here often."

"You mean there are others like this?"

"Of course. This one's more central, but it's not even the biggest. You should see Germini."

She rubbed her arms. "Maybe someday."

"The rec deck is pretty impressive, though. They have some new tech I've never seen before. Have you been there yet?" His smile faded when he noticed Ember's face. "Oh, that's right. I forgot that your father is sick. Of course you're not impressed by any of this."

She watched a soldier walk by, but the man didn't give them a second glance. “It’s just that he needs his medicine. Where do citizens go when they need to travel?”

“Uh, they don’t. It’s a military station, Ember. Those who leave go through inspections and all kinds of clearance, even the merchant pilots.”

She sighed.

“You know I’d help if I could,” he told her. “But even if it were possible, I’d be in huge trouble if they found out.”

“Oh, I bet.”

He checked his wristband, missing her sarcasm. “You look like you could use some cheering up. I want to show you something.”

“I’m not exactly in the mood for crowds,” Ember muttered.

“Not the rec deck. It’s something you can only find on this station, and not everyone knows it’s here. Come on.”

Stefan led her down several more corridors until Ember almost felt dizzy. How he knew his way around these drab white hallways was a mystery. On the sixth turn, Stefan suddenly whirled to face her, and she plowed into him.

He smirked. “You can walk next to me, you know.”

She felt her cheeks warm. In her village, it was inappropriate for a woman to walk in front of a man. She’d learned quickly to lag behind. “I’m more comfortable here.”

“Ah. Like the view, eh?” He winked.

“You’re insufferable.”

“Well, I’m a ladies-first kind of guy. But I’ll tell you what. Let’s meet in the middle, shall we? You can walk alongside me.”

Ember shook her head, feeling foolish, and stepped beside him. “Happy?”

“Quite.”

They continued to walk for another few minutes before the

hallway changed, opening up into a large room that looked to be some kind of public sitting area. A clear tube at the center carried people up and down. Soldiers and workers sat drinking and chatting at various tables. They seemed relaxed, almost content.

Obviously none of them had been torn from their homes in the middle of the night.

She caught a glimpse of a large hatch on the other side of the glass tube. She squinted at the words above it.

*Emergency Only.*

An escape pod.

"That's just a break room," Stefan said. He pointed to another corridor, but this one was lit with a strange blue light. "What I want to show you is down there."

She gave the escape pod one last glance. If there was one, there had to be others. Of course a station would have a way to get its residents to safety in case of an attack. She'd keep an eye out for more pod stations. If she managed to eject from here somehow, maybe she could hitch a ride home on a passenger ship.

Stefan led her to the entrance of the hallway, and she blinked in surprise. It wasn't a corridor but a small, dimly lit room with a sitting area. A huge screen spread across the opposite wall like a giant window.

"You have to sit down to get the full effect." Stefan plopped down in a seat and motioned to the one next to him. She gave him a coy look and sat two seats away.

"On," Stefan said with a crooked grin.

The massive screen flashed, and a scene took shape before her. It was like looking downward from the heavens. The camera stood atop an extremely tall mountain, so tall the clouds below were barely visible, and the ground not at all. Everything was green. No, an incredible array of greens, variations of the color she'd never even seen before. Several glass buildings shaped almost like castles soared high, even over the mountain peaks.

Figures moved slowly in the distance, as if they had all the time in the galaxy.

"What is this?" Ember breathed.

"Empyrean," Stefan said. "That's where you go when you've served the Empire well, kind of like retirement. The emperor himself lives there, as do most of his cabinet and the richest of citizens. Every edict and law comes from Empyrean."

So this was the Empyrean mentioned in the article. "Where is it located?"

"That's the thing. It's a closely guarded secret, as you can imagine. Security issues galore. Very few flickers have made a big enough impact to earn a spot there."

Ember couldn't tear her eyes away. It was so beautiful, so dreamlike. "You want to live there." Even she wanted to go, to enter those beautiful buildings and look down upon a world of green from the sky.

He paused. "Eventually. More than that, I want to earn a place there for my parents. A soldier who serves well enough can bring his whole family. And there's nothing my parents would like more than to live in the highest society in the universe."

She gave him a sideways look. What son sacrificed so much to help his parents reach a higher social class? Surely it went far deeper than love for his family. It had to be a personal challenge, something related to that vision she'd seen of him.

Ember tried to recall the details. The dead brother, the father whose dreams had just imploded. His lack of confidence in his younger son.

"Your brother was a flicker too," Ember said slowly. "So he served the Empire?"

Stefan's smile faded, and he looked at his hands. "He did, and flawlessly. Everyone thought Adam would make it to Empyrean someday, maybe even serve the emperor as a special assistant. But the Union had other plans. They sent assassins to target our flickers. Took out half our flicker force in a single night." His voice went hard at the end.

The Union again. That old man hadn't seemed like the brutal type, but then, she knew very little about them. The group must have been formidable, indeed, to threaten the Empire itself. "So he died in battle, and your parents thought all was lost. They forgot that their younger son had the same potential."

"I'll never be the flicker he was, and they know it." He took a deep breath. "Let's change the subject."

Ember turned back to the screen. "So you grew up on stations? Was that because of your father's work?"

"Nah. I was born on Gliesian System TX-31, but they took me from my parents when I tested positive for flicker ability at age sixty-two Gliesian months. They like to control how flicker children are raised. Too much potential for problems, as you can imagine. I've been training for this trip my entire life. Most of us have." He gave her an apologetic smile. "That puts you at a serious disadvantage."

"It would if I intended to stay."

He pressed his lips together in disapproval. "You aren't curious at all? You don't want to see how far you can go?"

"Nope, not really."

They sat there in silence, watching the screen for a long moment.

Stefan finally spoke. "Thanks for following me down here. Sometimes it's nice to get away from the others. They can get pretty draining after awhile."

She turned to face him. "But they're your friends."

"On the surface. Here, we're all competitors. It's just nice to talk to someone who isn't plotting how to beat me, you know? Actually, I think you know more about me than any of them, and I've only known you two days." He chuckled. "So what about you? When you get home, what do you plan to do? Assuming you can get that medicine to your dad."

She would live her life. Tell futures, help Bianca deliver her baby, help Dai recover, and try to forget what the Empire was doing with the others who held her gift. It was a simple life, but it was all she'd ever known. How could she explain that to a gadjo, especially a man raised by the Empire to become a weapon someday? He'd never understand.

"Whoa, slow down there. I can't keep up." Stefan chuckled.

Ember looked around the room, realizing how poorly lit it was in here. Had she really allowed herself to sit and talk with this man alone? Her father would be horrified at how far she'd fallen in two days.

She rose to her feet, smoothing the skirt that wasn't there. "Thanks for the tour. It's been . . . enlightening."

He stood, looking thoughtful. "You know, maybe you can mail that medicine to your dad instead of trying to escape. At least consider it."

Her wristband began to vibrate. It was nearly time for dinner.

*Just consider it.* Bianca's last words to her seemed like centuries ago. Dear Bianca. What did she think had happened to Ember? Was her friend caring for Dai in her absence, or was Mimi keeping her so busy she didn't even know Ember was gone? Had anyone thought to care for Dai, or did they rejoice at the thought of ridding themselves of the outsider at last?

*You will not die,* she told him inwardly. *Not yet, not now. I will find a way to get back to you, and we'll move on together like you wanted.*

"I'll walk you to the cafeteria," Stefan said, then hesitated. "Look, there's one last thing you should know. I'm going to give you a little more space once testing starts. I feel responsible for you being here, but, well, there are a lot of politics with this group. Everyone wants to graduate, so they'll do whatever it takes to beat out the others." He glanced at the screen, then down at the floor. "I come from a high family. That means the testers watch me more closely than most. If they think I'm helping you, it'll come back to hurt us both."

She absorbed his words. He hadn't mentioned Eris's name, but he wasn't fooling Ember as to his plea for space—he had a girlfriend, friends, and a plan. He didn't want Ember to get in the way.

It shouldn't bother her. She didn't care who he dated, because she'd be gone soon.

*The vision was wrong.* She would choose who she loved, and this man wasn't it.

"Then may the stars give you everything you desire." She turned and strode down the hallway, leaving him standing in the theater alone.

# 10

The cafeteria was one of the biggest rooms she'd ever seen in her life and was filled with ridiculously long tables. Stefan entered just after her, waved good-bye, and went to join his friends again. Ember filled her tray with the safest-looking food she could find. It smelled like some kind of mashed vegetable. She skipped over the meat and grabbed a water packet, then looked for an empty table.

A figure pulled up from a run at the doorway, breathing hard. Mar. The girl hesitated, then carefully tiptoed inside as if the doorway was some kind of dangerous, invisible border. When she saw Ember, her eyes narrowed.

*Stars.* She'd forgotten entirely about Mar.

Mar retrieved her tray, made her way to Ember, and slapped the metal tray down on the table. "Well?"

"Well what?"

"What happened to you? One second you were behind me, and then you disappeared. I thought you were lost in the city. I searched for another hour and a half."

Ember flinched. "Sorry. The pharmacist asked me to do a reading on her husband."

"That's it? What kind of excuse is that?"

"He was dying."

"We're all dying eventually. That's no excuse to blow off your friends." She plopped herself down on the bench across from Ember, scowling.

It was exactly what Bianca would have said. She was liking this girl more all the time. "You're right, it was very rude of me. I apologize."

"Well, next time tell me what's going on. I was really looking forward to that VR game." She frowned at the yellow mush on Ember's tray. "No meat, huh? I didn't take you for a vegetarian."

"I couldn't tell what it was."

She grimaced. "I know what you mean. But trust me, sometimes it's better not to know."

"It's not that."

Mar cocked her head. "Ah. It's a gypsy thing?"

"Roma, and yes. We don't eat meat that's . . ." She wasn't sure how to describe it. "Unclean."

Mar took a bite and chewed it thoughtfully. "I can respect that. What Earth animals are unclean?"

"Cats. Dogs, sometimes. Any animal that, you know, licks themselves."

"Well, I can guarantee none of this meat is a domesticated pet. We don't have any of those here. Most likely lamb, pennitt, or beef-flavored synthetic material. Sometimes they serve real chicken here, though. I hear the station has a good-sized poultry wing."

"Chickens are okay." She swallowed at the thought of her hens, probably starving as well. Or being eaten by her neighbors in her absence.

Mar shrugged and stabbed at her "synthetic material." "I know the Empire doesn't like differences, but I do. I think it's fascinating how people live. And my people have their own quirks." She looked up as if realizing Ember hadn't touched her food. "Do you need a fork?"

Ember shook her head. She'd grown too comfortable here with the *gadje*, and her upbringing was feeling more strange the longer she stayed. She'd obeyed the Empire's strict rules so far. She'd abandoned her beloved skirt and put on the horrid, overexposing trousers. But this was one thing she couldn't compromise on. Eating with utensils other *gadje* had used, placing them in her mouth, inside her body? She couldn't go that far.

She gave her tray a shake. The vegetable blob jiggled. She tilted it sideways, but the mass didn't slide at all. With a sigh, she scooped a bit into her hand and brought to her mouth.

*Ugh. Too sweet.* She forced the bite down and made a face.

As she ate, she recognized several of the languages being whispered around her, including Carbona and the more familiar Naravit'z, both languages her father had taught her. Although whenever a soldier walked by, they switched to Common. Most wore mint-green uniforms. Station workers, probably.

But something seemed strange about all this, something Ember couldn't put her finger on. It took her several minutes of watching the crowd before she realized what it was.

No children.

Her community was filled with them. They played and danced in the streets, shouting and screaming. Even the adults were loud. Each couple had several children, some as many as ten or twelve. Ember's only-child status was unusual, but her mother had had a medical condition that had prevented other births. The absence here felt like a gaping hole. Were there really no children on this station anywhere? What did parents do with their offspring, send them away or leave them behind?

Maybe some of these people didn't have children at all. Perhaps they were unmarried, alone. Like her. Maybe that was why they were here.

Everything about this place was unfamiliar and uncomfortable. Gone were the chickens underfoot, the lines filled with drying laundry, the smoke. Roma traveling about in their long skirts and braids. Her neighbors' nods as they walked by, however untrusting they were of Ember. Mothers calling for their children. Ember swallowed back the emotion closing her throat and swore she would find a way off this station once and for all.

"Look at your gypsy girl, Stefan," Eris called out from the other table, where the two sat side by side. "I told you they eat like dogs."

Stefan eyed Ember's fingers in confusion, but he recovered quickly. "And some people eat with sticks. Most of the people on my home planet drink their food from a bowl."

"And then there's ocean girl over there," Eris continued, completely ignoring Stefan's comment, "who can't handle walking into a room." She stood and wrapped her arms around herself. "Oh no," she said a mocking voice, "I have to pass through a doorway. Whatever shall I do?" She pretended to stick her toe over an invisible line, slowly and with agonizing care.

The others at their table laughed, except for Stefan, whose eyes blazed with disapproval. Mar simply poked at her food, but her cheeks had gone a deep crimson.

"Neither one will last long here," Eris said as she seated herself again. "I just don't understand why we had to travel so far out of our way just to investigate a tip that turned out to be a filthy gypsy girl. And a door-fearing Olvenack? Please. We haven't had an Olvenack flicker for a reason. Sometimes I wonder who makes these decisions." She snickered and tossed her hair.

"Eris," Stefan said in a warning tone.

Ember gripped the fabric where her skirt should be. Commander Kane had been investigating a tip? But who had told him? Dai was the only one who knew about her gift, and he would never have spread that around. She hadn't even known she was a flicker herself until the shuttle.

"Earth is highly overrated," Eris continued. "I can see why

humans left it behind. All that remains are the leftovers—the lazy, filthy trash nobody else wants. I don't get why they're even part of the Empire."

"Eris," Stefan snapped. "That's enough."

Ember felt anger hit her square in the stomach. She'd heard all these things before, but she wasn't in the mood today. She turned to face Eris and shot her a smoldering look. "Your great-grandparents gave us an entire planet so they could go live on a floating chunk of metal, Eris. Now we charge them to come back and visit the beach that used to be theirs. So who are the smart ones?"

"Your beach isn't that great," she snapped back, although her cheeks were pink now. "The water is too murky."

"Funny, you seemed perfectly fine with it the other day. I bet you didn't go in the water once. Do you even know how to swim?"

Eris's blush was a furious red now. She placed a dainty forkful of food into her mouth and tossed her hair if she hadn't heard. Stefan quickly changed the subject.

Ember turned back to her food, feeling her anger drain away. She didn't care what Eris said or did. Or Stefan either, for that matter. She finished off her meal and cleaned her hands on a napkin. Mar didn't say a word. She simply continued to pick at her food.

"Don't let Eris get to you," Ember finally said. "I've seen worse."

Mar sighed. "But she's right. There's a reason my people don't pass testing, let alone training. They see us differently." She looked up. "On my planet, we don't have doors. They're dangerous."

"How's that?"

"Our air is different. It reacts strangely to carbon dioxide, sometimes in poisonous ways. If a room is closed off with a person inside for too long, that person will die. And if you step inside right after the door opens—" She shuddered. "Hence, no doors. We don't even use walls, really. Just screens. Our homes are as open to the outdoors as you can get. I know it looks funny to everyone else, but I've just learned to be careful when I'm crossing rooms."

Ember was nodding. It made complete sense.

"Plus, I think the officers don't like us much," Mar whispered. "The last two Olvenacks, a twin sister and brother, sent word back to their family last year that they'd failed testing and would be sent home. But they never made it. It's like they just disappeared."

Stars. A tightness clutched at Ember's gut. "Is that what happens to those who fail?"

"Seems to be. The Empire makes it sound like they're too ashamed to return, but I've never heard of a failed flicker coming home. Ever." Her eyes bored into Ember's. "I'm terrified I'll end up just like them."

"Maybe they were having too much fun traveling and built new lives elsewhere," Ember offered, suddenly feeling a bit dizzy. She was determined to fail testing. Did that mean they'd make her disappear too? A week ago she would have doubted the theory, but having been kidnapped from her own home, she fully believed it was possible.

She'd just have to fail *and* make sure they sent her home. There was too much at stake.

Mar was still picking at her food.

Ember brushed the thoughts away and forced some cheerfulness into her voice. "If being a flicker is what you want, I'm sure you'll accomplish it. Shall we go find our quarters?"

"Absolutely." Mar stood and marched out with Ember, briefly pausing at the transition from cafeteria to corridor. As Ember gave the cafeteria one last look, she noticed Stefan watching her.

~

Ember's room wasn't too difficult to find. Mar's quarters were just across the corridor and three doors down. The girl gave her a friendly wave and went inside. By the smile on her face, Ember suspected she'd already put Eris's mocking behind her. Or maybe she was great at pretending.

The door to Ember's quarters whooshed open as she approached. Probably responsive to her wristband. She stepped inside, curious to see what Talon's gushing had been about.

The room was smaller than her bedroom at home, but the ceiling stood taller. A bed sat against the left wall and a desk in the other corner. Her mind registered the furniture with a single glance. All Empire-made, a hard plastic. An open door next to the desk revealed an automatic bucket—er, bathroom—much like the one on the shuttle and a tiny shower. But what really caught her attention was the window on the far wall.

She found herself walking toward it, mesmerized, as the door closed behind her. Instead of the dull-gray atmosphere she'd seen before, a glorious array of stars littered a black sky. Two satellites orbited in the distance like bright, moving stars.

Ember had seen the night sky many times on Earth, but she'd never seen it from space. Even the tiny window on the shuttle hadn't prepared her for this. She'd never felt so small, so utterly and completely alone.

When a tiny beep sounded from the desk, she tore herself away from the window and made her way over. A red light flashed on the desk's black surface. She tapped it, and an automated voice said, "Good evening, gypsy. What sounds would you like to play tonight as you sleep?"

*Gypsy?* Did they even care what her name was? Pushing away her irritation, she scanned the options. *Instrumental music. Hard music. Beach waves. Crickets and forest.*

She tapped the one that said "Rural" and was immediately comforted by the soft sound of clucking chickens. There were cows in the background instead of goats, but it was close enough.

*A nice room,* Ember admitted to herself. It had to be some kind of manipulation, a sample of the lavish lifestyle that awaited them if they succeeded in moving on to training. She threw herself onto the bed. For a military bed, it was surprisingly soft. Too soft. Her own mattress was made of straw and bits of cloth. All the gadje-made mattresses from before the exodus had rotted long ago.

She searched the room for cameras and found none. Eventually Ember yawned, feeling the day's events quickly catching up to her. Maybe she'd make it an early night.

"Lights," she said. The lights immediately clicked off. At least that kind of tech made sense.

A dull light radiated from the thousands of stars out her window. One of them, so far from here, was her home.

Tomorrow she would prove she didn't belong here. That meant failing whatever test they had planned in the morning. The Empire would send her home then. She'd make sure of it.

Ember removed her jacket and pulled a blanket over herself, letting exhaustion overcome her at last.

# 11

"Flicker testing, phase one," an automated voice said. "Deck 14, room B72. You are due to arrive in ten minutes." A pause, then it started over again. "Flicker testing, phase one . . ."

"Stop it," Ember groaned at the voice. There had to be a speaker in the wall somewhere next to her head for it to be this loud.

"Request denied. Deck 14, room B72. You are due to arrive—"

"Shut up."

"Request denied. Flicker testing, phase one." The voice was even louder now. She could make out the clucking of chickens and a sheep bleating. Had those sounds been going all night?

With a sigh, Ember swung her legs over the edge of the bed and stood on the cold floor. "There. Happy now?"

"Please confirm acknowledgment. Flicker testing, phase one—"

"Message confirmed!"

A pause. "Understood. Have a good day, gypsy."

She swore. "It's *Ember.*"

"Distinction noted." The room went silent, including the sheep and cow noises.

Ember had never understood the desire to replace a human being with artificial intelligence. Didn't that make a person irrelevant? Some looked down upon Ember and her profession, but it made her who she was. It made her valuable in some small way. She couldn't imagine designing a machine just to do readings on customers. Even if the robot somehow succeeded, what would she do in the meantime?

She turned to the window, expecting to see early morning sunlight. Instead she saw a solid wall of black with a few bright stars sprinkled in. On Earth, the sun had greeted her with its warmth in the morning. She'd basked in its comforting heat as the day went on. Even during summer months, it was the sun that kept their crop buildings running and their tourists coming. Waking to darkness left a pang of loneliness in her soul. Yet another thing her robot alarm clock couldn't understand.

"Time?" she asked the computer.

"0751, Gypsy Ember."

"Don't call me—" she began, then stopped. Nine minutes until phase-one flicker testing. The other flickers would be on their way there now, frantically trying to be on time. But that wasn't Ember. She was Roma, and she didn't belong here. Maybe it was time to drive that point home.

It was time for a little test of her own.

She slid her jacket on, wishing she had another outfit—anything besides this awful pair of trousers—and ran a hand through her hair. No time for brushing. Her stomach grumbled. Last night's dinner hadn't lasted her long. She'd have to figure out what some of these foods were. It wasn't like she could survive on vegetable mush forever.

She stepped out of her room to chaos. They'd put all the flickers together, it seemed, and she wasn't the only one running late. Several others in black jackets sprinted past her to the right, muttering curses under their breath. A bleary-eyed girl stumbled down the corridor, holding tightly to the rail along the wall. Eris. The girl threw her a pain-filled glance, then winced at the light and squeezed her eyes shut with a groan.

*Late night at the rec deck, princess?* Ember smirked, then remembered Eris had probably been with Stefan. Was Stefan this out of it too? No, he was too smart for that. He was probably there already, prepared to represent his family like a good son.

Ember took her time following them. The last one disappeared behind a corner, but still Ember took slow, lingering steps. She couldn't wait to see Commander Kane's face when she failed the program before it had even begun.

She looked around but didn't see another escape pod anywhere. It seemed she'd have to find the one near the break room from Stefan's tour yesterday.

Two wrong turns and fifteen minutes later she finally found it. The room was empty except for a woman sitting at a table, staring at nothing. Maybe she'd been there all night.

Ember approached the hatch and examined the sign overhead. *Emergency Only.* The hatch door was made of a strong, thick metal. There was also a yellow line on the floor, a half circle surrounding the hatch's immediate vicinity. She drew closer and leaned over it.

"STEP AWAY FROM THE POD," an automated voice said—a man's voice, sharp and loud. "SECURITY MEASURES ACTIVATED IN THREE, TWO . . ."

She leaped backward, and the countdown stopped. The woman who had been sitting earlier had leaped to her feet. She wore three pins in her collar and several patches on her uniform. An officer.

"Silly me," Ember said with a nervous chuckle. "Didn't mean to trip over that line."

"Try that again, and you'll deserve what you get," the woman snapped. She looked Ember up and down for a moment, then stalked away.

Ember examined the door again, looking for a weakness in its defenses. The sensors lined the entire width and length of the door. Taking out one or two wouldn't do it. She was considering trying again when the officer returned with two guards. They trotted in and stopped in front of Ember, stunners raised.

Ember stiffened. She should have waited for the woman to leave first. Maybe if she returned later . . .

"Hold out your band," the officer said. Ember complied and held her arm extended while the soldier scanned it.

"Just as I thought. You're supposed to be in phase-one testing right now, flicker. Deck 14, B-72." The officer gestured with her stunner. "We'll escort you. Someone has to make sure you get there without tripping over any more giant, clearly-marked emergency lines."

One of the guards snickered at the officer's joke, but he was tense as he took Ember's arm. Did touching a flicker make him so nervous?

The officer strode toward the clear lift tube. Ember raised an eyebrow. If they weren't arresting her, maybe her plan would actually work. Ember checked the time on her wristband. Surely she would have failed by now. She was almost twenty-five minutes late.

"I can't wait," she said.

Ember's escort shoved her forward, making her stumble. "She's one of yours," the officer snapped at the guard waiting outside the door. "We caught her testing out the security measures on escape pod 32."

"I got a little lost," Ember said.

"Right," the guard said sarcastically. He swiped his band and the door opened. "Get in there and find a seat."

Ember grinned. She hadn't even gotten a lecture. Maybe flickers were more feared than she'd thought. She filed the information away for later.

The meeting room was full of chairs filled mostly with bored-looking flicker recruits. Many of them turned toward the doorway, watching her with disapproval. There was no speaker, and the room was deathly silent.

"Interviews," the guard said behind her, as if reading her thoughts. "Sit." He shoved her inside, and the door closed behind her.

She ignored the watching eyes and found an empty seat, then settled in for a what she figured would be a long wait. She caught a glimpse of Eris sitting near the back, scowling at her. She seemed slightly more lucid now.

Six doors lined one side of the room, each with a single guard and a flicker waiting uncomfortably in front of it. Several empty seats were positioned at the front of the room, the first filled by a long-legged Talon. The chair was far too short for her, and her knees were practically folded up to her head, which gave her an eerie spiderlike look. The woman glowered at Ember.

It seemed the only people bothered by Ember's tardiness didn't have the power to do much about it. Her rebellion had been pointless.

The six doors began to open, and the next flickers were admitted. As they disappeared into what had to be a small, closet-sized room, Talon called out more names. Various flickers stood as their names were called, some shaky and nervous, others more confident. Ember rubbed the sleep from her eyes, wishing they could have scheduled a bit better. It would take hours for six interviewers to get through all these people. Why did they have to sit there and wait because of the Empire's poor planning? And what exactly was this supposed to accomplish? Surely the Empire already knew everything about each person. Stefan had said most were raised on stations preparing for this.

Mar crossed the room and sat next to her. "I can't believe you did that," she whispered. "Do you realize how dangerous that was?"

"What?"

"Getting here so late. I know you did it on purpose because I saw you standing in the corridor. I was almost late too." Her cheeks were still flushed, probably from her dash across the station.

Ember shrugged. "Nobody seems to care."

"Oh, the interviewers will care. They look for every opportunity to trim the numbers. There are only so many slots, and they give them to the higher families first." She sighed. "I can't decide which I fear more, failing or passing."

Six more names were called out. People stood and walked through the doors.

"Neither one sounds all that appealing," Ember admitted. She looked around the room at the nervous smiles and stiff postures of the other recruits. Stefan had called this a competition. Was Mar right about what failing meant? "I shouldn't be here."

"Yeah, well, the Empire obviously thinks otherwise." She sat back and sighed. "Let's talk about something else. My stomach is doing flips here. So what's it like to be a gypsy?"

"Roma," Ember corrected.

"You descendants of the Romans? I watched a special on the Roman Empire of Earth once. It was so interesting."

She paused. "Not exactly." That was a common mistake. Her people were travelers with blood from a dozen ancient countries. Ironically, they had very little Roman ancestry. She opened her mouth to explain it to Mar, but the girl had already moved on.

"I noticed Stefan has taken a liking to you." There was a question in her words.

Ember glanced across the room. Stefan was talking to one of his friends. He looked calm and unruffled.

"I never welcomed his attention," Ember muttered.

"Maybe that's why he likes you, then. Galaxy knows he's had enough women throwing themselves at him. Maybe you were a refreshing challenge."

*I didn't mean to get you in trouble*, Stefan had said. It was touching that he'd felt responsible, but irritating that he'd taken her under his wing like a lost baby chick—and then tried to distance himself from her.

*I don't care,* she reminded herself. *I don't need him, and I never will.*

Five more names were called, then a pause. "Gypsy."

"Sorry," Mar whispered as Ember stood. She wasn't sure whether the girl was apologizing for the lack of tact in the word *gypsy* or the fact Ember had been called up so early.

The guard practically shoved her inside the tiny room. Ember let her eyes adjust to the dim lighting. A table sat in the middle, with a chair on either side. Her interviewer had his hands folded on his lap.

Commander Kane.

## 12

"This is the one who was thirty-four minutes late, sir," the guard said from behind her. "Would you like me to send her with the failed group?"

"Not yet. Dismissed."

The guard complied, and the door slid shut, leaving Ember alone with the man who had stripped her of everything she loved. All the loneliness and worry she'd experienced over the past few days hardened, pooling into a single emotion. Anger.

"Sit."

She folded her arms and remained standing.

His mouth twisted, but he didn't pursue it. "You will answer my questions immediately and efficiently. Tell me your nationality, parents' names, their siblings, and any relatives, including cousins. Then we'll move on to your medical history."

The Empire already knew all that. This had to be a formality. "I'm not cooperating until you send me home."

He looked up from the tablet in his hands, his face darkening. This man wasn't used to being opposed. Something fluttered in Ember's stomach, but she forced herself to maintain eye contact.

However powerful Kane was, he couldn't force her to do anything.

"Home." He smirked. "Your chief gave you to me. I *own* you. I donated you to the Empire for testing. If you fail, you fall back into my hands."

The words stabbed her in the gut, but she stood her ground. "The first emperor outlawed slavery eighty years ago. You can't own a person."

The high commander gave her a long look, and for a moment Ember wondered if he would stand and strike her down. Surely he had the authority to do whatever he wanted. But he just leaned forward, his voice low and deep. "You can own a planet, gypsy girl. And those who own it, rule it. I have thirty thousand loyal citizens now, and they'd be happy to train you in my service. You're closer to failing than you know."

"I'm not what the Empire wants. I think we both agree on that. And I'm a free citizen of the Empire just like anyone else, so I'll be traveling to Earth with or without your permission."

Now his mouth tugged upward. "You really think failed flickers get sent home?"

She went stiff, struggling to keep her face impassive. "Why wouldn't they?"

The moment the words escaped her lips, she knew how naïve her question sounded. It was clear from the high commander's bemused expression that he was thinking the same thing. "Security issues," he said simply. "Not to mention the cost involved."

"So it's true. You kill flickers who fail."

He chuckled. "Of course not. They're useful in other ways, but we keep them under very tight security. We can't have failed flickers running around breeding and being snatched up by the enemy to use against us. It's hardly a secret that the emperor monitors your population very carefully for the safety of the realm."

"What other ways?" she demanded. "What do you do with—"

"Enough," he spat. "Your little stunt with the escape pod this morning is unforgiveable. You're fortunate you didn't try to open the door. You would have been killed on the spot. Now that you know what's at stake, you will answer my questions. Are there other flickers in your family?"

She fingered the container of medicine in her jacket pocket. Kane knew her father. She'd have to choose her words carefully. "I'm not a flicker. I just read the cards for tourists, that's all."

"Not a flicker?" He exhaled in a burst, almost like it was a chuckle. "Fine, I'll play your game, gypsy. You're going to predict my future just like you did for young Stefan a few days ago."

Had it only been days? It felt like months. "That was a performance. I made it up. Did a poor job of it, too."

"I spent twelve years scouting your kind as a seeker. I know a flicker when I see one, and your reading of young Stefan was impressive. Refuse me, and I will fail you here and now. Like I said, failed flickers have their purpose." He paused. "Particularly the women."

Nausea swept through her as she realized what the officer was suggesting. The anger that had pooled in her stomach began to leak into her blood now. She welcomed it, letting it expand and fill her with power. She would never belong to this man.

Fine. If failing wasn't an option, she'd just find another way off this ship and away from Kane's greedy clutches.

Ember closed her eyes and began to hum, but she wasn't gentle this time. She found his inner light and slammed into it, the memory of his sinister, suggestive smile singeing a hole into her mind. The light pulsed and fluttered.

She sifted through the man's memories. Five older brothers and a sister. A woman in a white uniform holding an infant. A funeral. The emperor's offer of a new position. Battle after battle. Kneeling at the emperor's feet, watching the old man's hands tremble with age. A more recent scene of Kane arguing with another high commander.

One light on the fringe pulsed brighter than the others. She reached out, hesitant, but the vision came to her before she could pull back.

*High Commander Lazarus Kane stood gazing out the window at the battle beyond. It was like a giant chessboard, this battle. It had taken him years of fighting to finally understand the truth of it. Every living being was just a pawn waiting to be placed wherever the master liked.*

*Today he was the master.*

*Lazarus smiled and lifted a single finger, then pointed it at the largest enemy ship.*

*He would have liked it to explode, but the lights in the windows simply flickered and died. The starboard thrusters went next. His fighters, seeing the massive ship's shields disabled, quickly swooped in to finish it off. Seconds later, a huge cloud of fire consumed the vessel.*

*He grinned again and pointed at the next ship.*

*The girl at his side flinched, but she was just another pawn too. An important piece. A queen, perhaps. He admired her slender form as she stood there, her dark eyes wide at the realization of what she had just done, her black hair falling forward into her face.*

*The emperor would be watching this battle with interest. He might even be excited at the prospect of ending the war in a single battle. But Lazarus's plans extended far beyond destruction of the enemy. There was a greater prize to be won than the bits of glory given at the old man's hand.*

Ember yanked herself out of the vision with a gasp. She was on the floor, her chair overturned.

The commander calmly looked down upon her, but his eyes were bright with excitement. "Do you always react so dramatically, gypsy?"

She sat on the ground, trembling. That terrible image of Kane standing next to the window wouldn't leave her—the way he'd pointed with no regard whatsoever for the lives he was taking.

And the very worst thing of all, the most horrifying twist she could imagine . . .

The girl at his side was Ember.

"Do you still deny your power, gypsy girl? It's obvious you saw something."

Ember's voice came out hoarse. She cleared her throat and tried again. "You glory in death. You—you *murder* people and call yourself a hero!"

He dismissed her words with a flick of the hand. "We're at war. The only difference between a hero and a villain is whose side you're on." He tapped his knuckles on the table, and the door whooshed open, revealing the waiting guard.

"Sir?"

"The girl appears a bit ill, so escort her to the medical bay. She was given a pill upon arrival, but I want a more thorough flush performed immediately."

"Yes, sir."

He turned on her. "Congratulations, gypsy girl. You've passed phase one."

# 13

Ember stumbled out of the medical bay, hand on the wall to hold herself up.

"Get back in here," the medic called out behind her. "You can't walk around for another twenty minutes."

She shook her head and straightened, burying the nausea inside her. "I'm fine." She wasn't. Ember had never been through such an invasive, terrible procedure. First they'd made her drink some horrible liquid, then she'd spent an hour in the bucket room—bathroom—vomiting. Along with the germs and bacteria, she also felt like she'd lost a liver and kidney.

Though that wasn't nearly as bad as witnessing that terrible man's future.

Her stomach churned at the memory, at the utter callousness Kane had displayed. She wished her mind could be cleared rather than her body. Her vision of Stefan kissing her was nothing compared to this.

Surely the stars were wrong about what awaited her. If she could just get home, none of it could happen. She had to focus on her goal.

But not right now. She just wanted to go back to her room and disappear into a blissful sleep. Even now her stomach was unsteady enough that she never wanted to eat again. Thank the stars she'd skipped breakfast.

Holding on to the rail, she slowly made her way down the corridor leading to the lift near her quarters. Two hallways later, she caught the scent of food and realized how near she was to the cafeteria. It was just ahead—and so was another trip to the bathroom if she didn't get away from the smell. Holding her nose, she stumbled past the double doors.

"Hey, you passed." Stefan approached and halted abruptly when he saw her face. "Whoa. What happened?"

She gritted her teeth. Why now, of all times? "Commander Kane felt a flush was in order."

"Ah." He nodded sympathetically. "I went through that when I was eight. By the look on your face, I'm guessing they haven't improved the process any."

She gripped the side rail more tightly and shook her head.

"I'll help you to your room." He took her arm and draped it over his shoulder. Somewhere from deep beneath the nausea, she realized Stefan was more toned than she'd thought.

*No,* she reminded herself. She was going home to marry a respectable Roma man. The future her gift had revealed could never be. Not if it meant fulfilling Kane's future as well.

"But you'll miss lunch," she managed.

"I already ate."

A lie. He'd been heading toward the cafeteria, not away from it, but she didn't have the strength to argue. It was clear she'd never make it to her room on her own.

He placed his other hand on her waist, sending a shower of tingles up her spine. He was now supporting most of her weight.

"Is this all right?" he asked, sensing her discomfort. "I guess I could carry—"

"No," she barked. "This is fine."

"I was going to say I could help carry you to find a hover-chair," he said, "but if this works . . ." He grinned as he continued to help her move forward.

It was several minutes before they reached the wing where the flickers' quarters were situated. The silence between them was heavy yet comfortable. He seemed to sense that Ember wasn't in the mood to talk. Two flickers Ember recognized from yesterday walked past them with raised eyebrows. Stefan greeted them casually, as if he escorted sick girls home all the time.

When they finally reached her door, she extracted herself from his arms and stood shakily on both feet. They held this time, but her nausea still threatened to manifest itself.

"I found a shipping department on deck thirty-three central," he whispered. "In case you still need to mail your package. Not sure how expensive it is, but hopefully they deliver to Earth. I know you're worried about your dad."

"Thirty-three," she repeated. "Thanks."

The bitterness in her voice must have been evident, because he waited until a group of workers passed before he spoke again. "I know you don't want to be here. But since you are, why not explore a bit? I've been meaning to ask if you wanted a tour of the recreation deck."

"I thought you wanted to stay away from me."

His smile faded. "I didn't mean it like that."

"You feel guilty. You feel responsible for me being stuck here. Is that it?"

"No. Well, yes, but—"

"If you're worried I'm mad at you, just forget it. Go impress your friends and pass their tests and become a better flicker than your brother. You don't have to prove anything to me."

His thick eyebrows drew together in a grimace. "Did it ever occur to you that I didn't want anyone to know about Adam? From the moment they dragged you onto the ship, my friends haven't stopped asking me questions." He released a long breath, then spoke more slowly. "Look, I'm not here to impress anyone,

Ember. I'm here because I want to serve the Empire. Because I believe in it. The Empire isn't perfect, but it's better than the way things were before."

"It's better for *you.* Not for everyone."

"You honestly believe Earth would be better off without the Empire? It wouldn't even exist. The scavengers would have destroyed it long ago."

Stefan knew more about her planet than she'd guessed, but she wasn't ready to give in yet. "They don't come around very often. We could fight them off if the Empire would allow us weapons."

"I thought you were a peaceful people. That's what the info screens say." He cocked his head. "Although having known you a few days, I'd say that couldn't be further off."

"Very funny." The door opened, but she hesitated. "Info screens, you say?"

His defensiveness went back up. "I looked up the history of your people last night. I needed some good reading."

Interesting. She couldn't help but wonder what the Empire thought of the Roma people. Ember knew a little of her own town's history, but it was hard to get specifics from the elder Roma. All she knew was that the Roma had been left behind during the great exodus. Once everyone left, they had traveled from the desert to the coast, where the land was more fertile. They'd taken over the agricultural buildings and now grew their own food, but their fertile land and freshwater were growing more scarce as Empire's restrictions grew.

"So the info screens are on the recreation deck?" she prodded.

"I thought that might catch your attention. If you meet me tonight, I'll show you how they work." He sighed. "Well, I have something right after dinner, so let's meet there around 20:00, if you think you'll be up to it. Deck 59. There should still be screens available that early. If we wait until later, the gamers will stake their claim and play all night."

She nodded despite herself. "Fine." If these info screens had information about her people, maybe they had current news as well. "And thanks for the tip about the shipping department. I didn't think you'd actually help me."

"Help you? I don't know what you're talking about." He threw her a mischievous grin. "I'll see you tonight, then."

Deck thirty-three looked just like every other deck until Ember reached the central packaging unit. The woman at the desk was on a call, talking so fast Ember could barely understand her. The lady thumbed through the virtual file hovering in front of her, its outline barely visible. She finally closed the call with a quick "Yes, ma'am" and turned to Ember, looking her up and down. "What?"

"I need to ship something," Ember said.

"You're a flicker." The words darted out of her mouth so quickly Ember almost didn't catch their meaning.

Ember raised an eyebrow, unsure what the woman wanted her to say. "Yes?"

"Officers don't send flickers to run errands, so this must be a personal issue. This is a military station, with military personnel and vehicles. We don't ship things for soldiers."

"But—"

"I don't care if your baby brother is dying or your best friend is committing suicide or your planet is about to explode. And believe me, I've heard it all. I can't take whatever it is you want to send. You'll have to wait for reassignment on a civilian planet. Some mercenary will be happy to take care of it for you."

Ember took a deep, frustrated breath. "You don't understand."

"No, *you* don't understand. Using military resources to send a personal package is illegal—against the law, punishable by imprisonment, unethical, and in nowise allowed. Now leave me to my work." The woman turned back to the screen and began fumbling with it again.

"I shouldn't be here," Ember said quietly. "They kidnapped me. My father desperately needs this medicine on Earth. There must be something I can do."

The woman tensed, her fingers pausing midair. "Did you say Earth?"

Ember nodded.

Fast-talking lady muttered something under her breath and began her fumbling again.

"Excuse me?"

"Talk to Ambrose," she repeated, her voice barely audible. "Short, fat guy who comes in once a day. He hasn't been in yet, so if you wait in the hall, you might catch him. Now stop looking so hopeful. There's a camera above your head, you know."

Ember let her shoulders slump as if disappointed, then turned toward the door. But inside her heart was leaping. *Ambrose.*

It was her smuggler—the one who visited Earth once a month for deliveries. Even better, he was still here. She was willing to forgive him for standing her up if it meant he could help her now. The man had a ship somewhere on this planet where he stored his illegal cargo. Surely there was enough space for her on that ship. And if he refused to take that risk, he could at least deliver Dai's medicine for her until she got home.

Ember stood in the hallway for a while, bouncing on her toes and pacing to contain her excitement. After forty minutes, her frustration had ceased to become an act—she was supposed to meet Stefan any minute now. She could hear the woman inside bidding her coworkers farewell. The dock was closing for the night.

She checked her wristband for the sixtieth time and sighed. Another day wasted. Tomorrow would bring another test, another humiliation, another day under that dreadful man's thumb. Ember had showered the moment she'd returned to her room, trying to wash the filth of his vision away, but she still felt the taint on her soul.

Ember would come back tomorrow. And the next day. Whatever it took to meet Ambrose, she would do it. He would make everything right.

She gave the shipping door one last look, then trotted toward the lift.

# 14

Ember was blasted with the sound of loud music as the lift opened onto the rec deck—at least she thought it was supposed to be music. It thumped through her soul in a harsh, sharp way. Not at all beautiful or poetic. The crowd mingled, bodies dancing to the sounds pumping through the wall speakers. And the way they combined themselves—it just seemed wrong. Men and women dancing together. They couldn't all be married.

Ember scanned the room and found the info-screen booths on the opposite wall. She'd have to push through the crowd to get there. If Stefan was correct, the crowd would only get bigger—and drunker—as the night wore on. She didn't see Stefan anywhere. If he was dancing, she'd never be able to distinguish his face from the hundreds of other faces under the colorful lights.

She stepped into the pool of writhing bodies, grimacing as she received an elbow to the face. Halfway through, someone stepped on her foot, but eventually she managed to reach the other side. The lighting here was blue, bathing everything in an eerie, cold hue. A few screens were set into the walls, and people sat in front of them, bizarre-looking goggles on their faces.

She chose an empty screen and sat but didn't put the goggles on. Instead, she touched the screen.

"What can I do for you?" the automated woman's voice said in Common. No language options, of course. A display of options appeared at her fingertips. She read through them slowly, wishing she'd practiced her Common a bit more thoroughly. *Entertainment. Games. News. Music videos. Education. Research.*

She tapped the last one, and a huge menu appeared. She scanned through the items until one caught her eye. She selected it and sat back to watch, breathless. Was this really stored here for anyone to see?

*The Exodus of Earth*

Images appeared with text, and she leaned right up against the glass, trying to take it all in. She read as quickly as possible, absorbing all she could. Skimming through the names and dates, she looked for specific keywords. When they didn't appear, she typed them into the search option, then sat back impatiently. The results came up immediately, and she opened them.

She began reading and snorted in disgust. "You're kidding me."

"You figured out how to work it," Stefan said, carrying two drinks and handing her one. "I figured a Sansori was a safe bet. If you don't like it, I'll get you something else." He sat beside her. "You're looking up the history of your people?"

"This *isn't* our history." Her voice was hard, but she couldn't help it. "At least, this isn't the way it really happened."

"Kind of hard to deny photos," Stefan said, then took a long sip.

"This says everyone left because the planet was dying. This says a new world was found, a larger one with more freshwater and fertile land. It was better in every way, and everyone was invited, no matter their nationality or race."

Stefan nodded. "That's true. My great-great-grandfather was one of them. He left on the thirty-eighth ship."

"This also says the Roma declined and opted to stay behind." Ember said. "That's not true. We tried to leave, but they wouldn't let us."

Stefan lowered his glass. "Is that what your people believe?"

"It's what we know. They left us behind, refused to allow us passage. We moved to the coast and took over the abandoned agricultural buildings. It wasn't until a celebrity visited and proclaimed our beach the best in the universe that tourists began coming back." She frowned. "I don't think you would find us well off, but compared to before, we have everything we need."

"Funny how history depends on who's telling it." Stefan took another long sip. "My instructors always said Earth is a dying planet, that some groups are pushing to have it discontinued. That it requires too many Empire resources to protect. Even my dad thinks it's too far and we need to consolidate our military forces, especially with the Union gaining power."

Ember wasn't surprised. Her father had grumbled about this a few times, and she'd heard tourists talk about it. But it was just talk. It had to be.

"And you?" she asked. "What do you think?"

"I think it's a fascinating planet with a beautiful history and culture. It needs to be preserved as a historical monument, if nothing else. I mean, most of the beings in the universe can trace their ancestry back to Earth." He smiled and took another sip. "The land is a little harder and drier than on my planet, though. Gliesian ground is kind of soggy. You have to wear boots or a nasty fungus will get your toes. But it's ideally placed, so the Empire favors it."

"You don't seem to miss it much."

He shrugged. "It was never home to me, not really. The Empire took me to preflicker training pretty early. I don't remember much before that—my parents talking, my mom tucking me into bed, playing with swamp bugs in the backyard. That kind of thing."

"It's the people you miss," she said, thinking of Dai and Bianca. "Not necessarily the place. Didn't your parents ever come visit you?"

He pressed his lips together, and she instantly felt bad for asking. She already knew the answer. She'd seen the way his parents looked at him, as if he were an untrained pet who had already disappointed them. It was the elder son they'd loved, the one who would ever remain perfect in their hearts. Not the struggling, grieving son who needed them most.

"Listen," she began. "I'm sorry for what I said about your brother."

His face darkened, but he ignored her apology and motioned to her glass. "It's worth a try. I know it's not what you're used to, but it'll give you a nice buzz."

Ember sniffed her glass, happy for the change of subject. It smelled of overripe pineapple and something salty. Satisfied, she stuck the straw inside and began to gulp it down. It wasn't as strong as she liked, but it did have a pleasant, fruity taste. She quickly finished off the drink, then set the glass back on the desk.

Stefan's eyes followed it. "Whoa. I've never seen someone chug a drink through a straw before."

Ember scanned through the rest of the article and flipped through the last two mentions. No news. Everything was historical.

Finally she closed it and turned to Stefan. He seemed content to be with her today when yesterday he'd practically avoided her. What was his motive? If this truly was a competition, he had to have one.

"Is that all you wanted me to see?" she asked.

He sputtered. "Well, there's a lot more to do than study history. You can play VR games on here. You just put the goggles on—"

She eyed the goggles with contempt.

"Or," he said quickly, "I think there are a few card tables out there. Maybe a pool table or two."

"A pool?" Ember asked, suddenly curious. She missed the feel of water on her skin. She'd even accept sitting next to the water, tasting it on the air. Mar had been right about that, at least. The lack of ocean simply felt wrong to a girl who swam whenever tourists weren't around.

"Uh, no. It's a game where you hit balls with long sticks. Water is too valuable a resource to waste letting people play in it. People would just steal it and bring it home."

"Oh." She swallowed her disappointment. "Are there musical instruments anywhere here?"

"Music," he repeated, looking thoughtful. "As a matter of fact, yes. Follow me."

He led her through the crowd, weaving easily around the dancers. It seemed everyone on the dance floor knew Stefan. A few of the women grinned invitingly when they saw him, but he just waved. They scowled when they noticed Ember at his side. She didn't see Eris anywhere.

Ember froze at the sight of one of the dancing figures near the edge, a man. He was shorter than her and wore a beard that covered much of his neck, which made him stand out in the military crowd. She'd know that beard anywhere.

Ambrose.

Ember bolted toward the man and slid to a messy halt in front of him. "Ambrose! I need to talk to you."

The man's eyes widened, and he looked frantically around as if embarrassed his friends might hear. "Excuse me?"

She remembered where they were and leaned forward. "I need a favor. It's urgent."

"Do I know you?"

"Ember," she hissed into his ear. "We've met several times,

remember? I need you to take me to Earth, to the landing pad by the Roma village."

"Roman? What are you talking about, girl? I can barely hear you."

"The, uh, gypsy village. Can you take me there?"

The man's eyes narrowed, and the woman dancing next to him finally realized they'd been interrupted. She stopped swaying and focused her gaze narrowly on Ember. "What's going on?"

"Please," Ember said. "It's an emergency. I'll give you all I have and more."

"Wait," the woman said, looking suspicious. "Ambrose? Who is this girl?"

"Nobody of consequence," Ambrose said, his thick eyebrows furrowing into one long line of hair. "One of my trainees at the office had an object for me. We made a bet, you see. The prize plus my winnings. What was the amount again?"

He'd slightly emphasized the word *object.* He only smuggled nonliving cargo. The disappointment hung bitter in her chest. Time for plan B. "Two hundred and nineteen credits." She programmed the payment into her wristband and held it out.

He accepted the payment without hesitation. "We also had something else involved in the deal, did we not?"

Irritation boiled in her chest. "A hen," Ember said, thinking quickly.

Amusement touched his expression.

She jumped in again. "Four hens. All healthy." She hoped. There was a very good chance her neighbors had eaten them already, but she had nothing else of any value to this man. "The owner's name is Nicholae."

"Chickens," he muttered. "Fair enough. I suppose I can consider our transaction completed." He offered his arm for a handshake. Ember slipped the pill bottle into his palm, and he discreetly closed his fingers around it and slipped it into his pocket.

"Thank you," she breathed, feeling much lighter already. "Thank you so much."

He turned back to his date. "Chickens," he said again, and she laughed.

When Ember reached the lift, Stefan was waiting with a strange expression on his face, but he didn't ask why Ember had left him. As the doors slid closed behind them, Ember melted against the wall in relief. She had done it.

Her father would get the medicine soon. All would be well.

Minutes later, they stood in a small room with a stage and rows of empty chairs. Instruments lay against the walls, although they looked to have been discarded for good reason. Most were broken right in half, while it appeared the others had fallen into disrepair over time.

"A recital hall," Stefan said. "Every station has one, but music creation isn't something the Empire emphasizes anymore. Takes too much time, too many resources."

A familiar story. Ember eagerly scanned the available instruments, but her excitement fizzled. Several chrome pieces, an electronic piano, and a couple of wooden instruments with strings. Not an accordion or cimbalom in sight. She stepped over to what looked like a large, squat violin propped against the stage and picked it up by the neck. "What's this?"

Stefan looked surprised. "A guitar. An earth instrument. I thought you'd be familiar with it."

She strummed her fingers across the strings. The sound was strange, too bright. She put it down, ready to give up the trip as fruitless. Then she spied a hand drum on the ground. She took it into her arms and thumped it with the palm of her hand, nodding in satisfaction.

"The men in our village play while the women dance," she said. "I'll show you the rhythm."

He choked and sat forward in the chair he'd just lowered himself into. "Oh no. I don't play. I've never touched an instrument in my life."

Ember didn't push the issue. Instead, she sat on the edge of the stage across from Stefan and began to accompany the song unfolding in her head. Two deep beats and a fluttering, like a bird in flight. Ember closed her eyes, allowing the tune to take form in her throat. Then she released it in the form of a hum, the words coming next.

*Tree climber, tree climber, high in the sky*
*You are rooted in the tree you climb*
*Deep in the earth you love.*

*The life flowing beneath your hands*
*Pulses also through tree veins, insects, plants*
*Through all things living and touched by life.*

*Deny not the death that has spread*
*For just as the sky extends*
*So does the ground, deep-rooted and strong.*

*The same flame you carry within*
*Is the life that binds us all.*
*The light that binds us all.*

She let the rhythm drain from her fingertips as she held the last note. Then she opened her eyes.

Stefan's mouth hung slightly open. He cleared his throat. "Uh, that's the song you hum when you do readings. I recognize it."

"It's the only song I know in Common," she said. She held out the drum again. "Your turn."

"Oh no. My talents lie elsewhere. Can you—can you sing it again?"

Ember had sung this song for tourists before as a child, dancing for tips as visitors watched silently from the sidelines. She had always loved its wistful tone, its painful longing, and the warmth she felt when she became one with the lyrics. But her mother had told her to stop after awhile. It had taken her years to understand why. *Gadje* music was harsher, more grating on the nerves, with lyrics that fell hard on the ears. Tourists wanted to move, not be moved.

The fact that Stefan felt the same magic she did sent a pleasant tingle down her arms.

She nodded and sang the song again. This time she let herself sway to the music, wishing her father were playing so she could give the song proper observance with a dance.

Stefan looked thoughtful as she finished. "The life flowing beneath your hands pulses also through . . . I can't remember. What's the line?"

"Tree veins, insects, plants," Ember continued. "Through all things living and touched by life. It's a traditional song from centuries ago. My father taught it to me to help me learn Common."

"Reminds me of the inner light," he said. "You don't suppose your people knew about it even then?"

Ember stroked the hand drum, feeling the softness of the fabric stretched tight across the top. It wasn't true animal skin but something unfamiliar. "I'm sure they did. We've been reading futures for centuries. Maybe even a thousand years."

"Interesting. Scientists have come up with all kinds of theories as to where flickers came from. Did you know the one common ancestral thread is Earth? The problem is, we've spread ourselves so thin it's hard to find someone who doesn't have Earth blood in them. I've heard theories about flickers originating with the Mayans. Others insist it was the Native Americans." He leaned forward. "What if it was the gypsies all along?"

"Roma," Ember corrected.

"Sorry. Roma." His excitement only grew. "This is so fascinating. I'd love to meet your people, Ember. I want to know more about them. And I'd really like to learn more about you."

Ember carefully set the hand drum down and stood, a twinge of worry forming in her stomach. "I think it's time to retire for the night."

"Look," Stefan said. "I need to tell you something. Just hear me out."

"No, my turn first. The viewing of Empyrean, the drinks, and now the music. Everywhere I go, you're there. I want to know why."

He looked taken aback. "Must there be a reason?"

"Yes, and I think you're hiding it from me."

Stefan finally met her gaze, holding it firmly. "Maybe I feel bad for what happened and I'm trying to make it up to you."

"Possibly, but I doubt it."

He sighed. "Look, I don't have any ulterior motives. I never did, even that first day. I didn't ask you to read my future because I was making fun of you. It's because when I saw you sitting there in that market, I remembered something my grandmother said a long time ago."

Ember wasn't sure what she'd expected, but it wasn't that. She sat down across from Stefan again, folding her hands, ignoring the nervous flutter in her stomach. "Go on."

"I can't believe I'm telling you this." He sat back in his chair and crossed one leg over his knee. "It happened when I was a boy.

I'd just been accepted to flicker pretraining. My parents threw a party for their friends and relatives the night before my departure. While they were drinking themselves under the table, my grandmother pulled me aside and said she was a flicker too but she'd never told anyone. She offered to read my future, saying it would help her feel better about me leaving."

Ember nodded. His grandmother sounded much like her father.

"My grandmother told me I would someday meet a fierce girl with black hair and tan skin. She said that girl would refuse to conform to the Empire and would shape the universe around her instead. She also said I would help her do it." He looked at the ground, his face coloring. "I forgot all about her prediction until I saw you in that market."

Ember hesitated. "You know that could be anyone, right?"

"Of course. But what are the chances that you'd be a flicker? And that we both ended up right here, on the same station at the same time? The odds are almost astronomical."

"I know you want to read something into this, and I don't blame you, but, Stefan, I can't stay. I have to get back to my father."

He looked away. "So you've said. Many times."

"I don't mean to hurt you. I just have other plans for my life. Plans that involve my own people and my family. None of them involves the Empire or the military or . . . killing people. I believe the stars gave us these gifts to be used for good." The words sounded hypocritical in her ears. Here she was, lecturing a man who had probably never killed anyone in his life. Not like her.

"What if this is *why* you have your gift? Think of what two flickers working together could accomplish." His voice was pleading now. "We could change things, make the Empire more accepting of distant cultures and languages. Maybe nudge the flicker program in a different direction. You could make a huge difference here."

He leaned toward her. Ember caught a whiff of soap from his slightly messy hair. Stefan's chin was covered in stubble, and she wondered what it would feel like to brush her fingers along his jawline. She gripped her hands more tightly together at the thought.

"Please don't rush off yet," he whispered. "I don't think this is an accident. I really believe you're here for a reason."

Ember sucked in a long breath, attempting to send oxygen to her light-headed brain. His closeness did something strange to her. Even worse, she really liked it.

She had to get out of this place, and soon.

She rose to her feet and tore her gaze away, breaking the connection. "Even if you're right, my father is my priority right now." *I took my mother away, and now I have to take care of Dai as she would have.* "I'm sorry."

Stefan stood as well, his mouth twisted in disappointment.

There was a long silence as neither spoke.

Finally Stefan broke the silence. "Sounds like you know what you want. I won't get in your way. If you're ready to go, I'll walk you back to your room."

# 15

For the second night in a row, Ember didn't sleep well. She awoke the next morning to the sound of bleating sheep. She yelled to the AI to discontinue the sounds, trying to remember whether she'd requested background noise last night. Maybe the AI was feeling particularly facetious this morning.

Ember had barely enough time to grab a quick pastry from the cafeteria before phase-two testing began. She arrived on time and seated herself with the rest of the flickers. Nearly a third of them had been eliminated at the interview round, leaving a bunch of empty seats. She was curious to know what had transpired in their interviews to knock them out of the running. Had the other officers required a demonstration of them as well?

She looked around, noting that it was almost identical to yesterday's, except that there was only one door instead of six.

Talon stood and explained that today's testing involved some kind of machine. Flickers would be called in one at a time. Ember did the math and sighed inwardly. They'd be here a long while again. At least it would give her time to plan her escape.

Failing the test wasn't an option anymore, not with Kane so

determined to make her a slave. The escape pod was out until she figured out how to get past its defenses. Besides, she didn't know how to program a pod even if she did manage to eject it.

That left finding another cargo ship to hide away on. She didn't even know where to begin. Mar had said the Empire stored their ships below the planet's surface. But how did she get down there, and where would she find a pilot?

She caught a glimpse of Stefan near the front. Eris sat next to him, her head resting on his shoulder. The sight sent an odd pain through her. He'd cited politics as his reasoning for those particular friends, but she didn't understand why he put up with Eris. What was so special about her? The girl acted as though she owned the station, and most everyone she met seemed to agree with the sentiment.

*You rejected Stefan,* she reminded herself. *You have no one to blame but yourself.*

She was the fourth flicker to be called up by Talon. "Ember Gypsy."

"Getting closer," Ember muttered. The guard opened the door, and she slipped inside. Instead of shutting softly behind her, it slammed with a metallic *clang*. It was lined.

The lights were dim, like in yesterday's interview room. A tall machine much like a booth stood in the center of the square room, its opening barely wide enough to admit one person. A dark, one-way mirror lined the far wall, and a guard stood at attention to the left.

She reached out mentally to feel who sat on the other side of the mirror. It was difficult to penetrate the specially-lined walls, but she managed to sense six flickering lights in a small booth, all officials, none of them Kane.

"Ember Gypsy," a woman said on the speaker. "Step inside the machine."

"Roma, not gypsy," Ember said automatically. "And first I want to know what it does."

She could sense the woman's light increase in brightness. Anger. Did the other flickers really obey so blindly? It could be a deathtrap, for all she knew.

"It assesses your abilities," the official finally said. "It's perfectly safe, I assure you. Step inside."

The guard looked ready to toss her in. She glared at him as she slid into the narrow machine.

The machine whirred as the door closed, and then she was left in complete darkness.

"Please wait," the official's voice said. It was more distant now, fed into a smaller speaker near Ember's right ear. "Someone is walking into the room now. This person will stand in front of the machine. You'll reach out and try to read his or her immediate future. What you see will be transmitted for everyone else to watch."

Such incredible technology. She was awed by the possibilities until she realized what the Empire would want to use it for.

She sensed another light entering, someone entirely different from the watching officials. Another woman, unfamiliar.

"Whenever you're ready, Ember."

She closed her eyes and reached out with her mind, but the machine made it difficult to grasp the light. Too much interference. They were probably testing her strength. She mentally reached for it again only to have her hand move right through the flame. Ember frowned, then released a long sigh and began to hum her song, the music helping her to focus and to forget where she was.

She reached out once more, and the vision came.

*Liza Hosler trembled in her father's embrace. She must be strong like he wanted. She blinked back the threatening tears and stood straight, just like they'd practiced.*

*"You be good," her father said as he pulled back to examine her. "I'll come visit you soon."*

*"When you're on leave?"*

*He winked. "Of course. What other lovely lady would I visit?"*

*Her eyes were growing blurry with moisture, and she blinked more rapidly. "I'm afraid of that school. Please don't send me there."*

*"Oh, honey." He pulled her in against his chest, holding her tight and resting his chin on her head. She took in the scent of him. It felt like home. "I know it's not what you're used to, but it's the safest place for you right now. That's why I have to go—to make home safe for you again."*

*"And then you'll come back."*

*"Absolutely." He kissed her forehead and stood. "They'll take you to your new room, and you'll get to meet Miss Borringer. She taught me when I was your age. I think you'll really like her. Okay?"*

*"Okay." Her voice barely quivered that time.*

Ember shuffled to another memory and let the vision fade. A new one surfaced.

*The letters on the shiny metal walls all ran together in her mind. Sheet after sheet of them, name upon name. All words representing lives taken much too soon. There was a reason she never visited the memorial planet. She couldn't quite grasp the magnitude of it all.*

*There. One metal sheet read "The Heroes of the Battle of Narrad."*

*She filled her lungs slowly, frozen where she stood. She didn't have to look. Maybe it would be better not to know. She could pretend he was still at war somewhere, that he'd never been taken by the enemy. That he would be home soon.*

*Her unconscious mind took control before she could stop it, scanning the names until one seemed a hundred times larger than the rest.*

*"Benjamin Hosler."*

*The tears should have come then, hot and full of a decade of pain, loneliness, and uncertainty. That was what she'd expected from this visit. But now that she knew the truth, there was nothing. Just a deadness inside. She'd left her tears behind in a childhood that no longer existed.*

Ember heard a strange sound, the mix of a gasp and a sob. Then the official's voice spoke again. "You're upsetting the host, Ember. We want the future, not the past."

They didn't understand. When she made a connection, she experienced everything. It was all-encompassing. She couldn't move half a finger without affecting the other half. They were all parts of the same being.

She ignored her irritation and went deeper into the less-certain light, the part that flickered and popped like a dying fire.

*Liza Hosler stood in front of the machine, shuffling her feet uncertainly. She had volunteered to do this because it meant a break from the shipping job she hated, and at first it had been interesting enough. Memories she'd long since buried flashed across a screen on the outside of the machine. But now, as she watched the machine before her begin to glow, she regretted her decision.*

*The white metal pulsed as if with an inner light. She could see the outline of a person inside, like a shadow in front of a flame. The screen began to flash, and lines appeared. This hadn't happened with the previous three candidates she'd hosted.*

*Liza looked at the mirror impatiently. Any second now the officials would intervene. They had promised to keep her safe from the flickers. But they were certainly taking their time. The machine had begun to turn a warm orange color now.*

*"I think—" the official began, but she was interrupted by a terrible noise. Liza watched, stunned, as the screen's glass began to crack.*

*"Stop," the official cried over the speaker. "Gypsy, stop this instant."*

*The screen's crack began to spread like a web over the glass. The images ended, but the machine continued to glow. It was a soft pink now.*

*"Stop it," the official shouted. "End this now!"*

"Now!" the woman cried.

Ember's eyes flew open. Her entire body felt like it was melting beneath her clothing, and her exposed skin burned. She yelped and shoved at the booth's tiny door, but it wouldn't open.

Voices sounded from the room outside as Ember sucked the overheated air into her lungs. What had just happened?

The door finally burst open, and a wave of precious, cool air washed over her. She stumbled out, falling to the floor at a guard's feet. All six officials gaped at her from the protection of the far doors. Even the woman she'd just read, Liza, stared at Ember as if she were the devil incarnate.

"What was that?" a man with white hair muttered from the doorway.

"That wasn't the future," another woman pointed out. "Seeing the present isn't what we're looking for."

"Plenty of flickers have seen the present. None of them has broken the machine like that. I mean, look at it."

Ember turned and choked. The metal booth barely stood upright, it's walls melted as if made of wax. She rose to her feet and stumbled away, panting.

The female official glowered at her. "This machine is incredibly expensive and difficult to replace. Tell me what you did and why."

It would definitely need to be replaced. It looked like a partially melted candle. "I didn't do anything," she said. "I—I don't know what happened."

The officials exchanged a look.

"It's obvious," the first man said. "She got inside the wiring somehow."

Another official spoke up. "Impossible. The wiring panel is on the outside, near the back."

"Well, gypsies are good with their hands. I wouldn't put it past her to damage the machine on purpose. She's been nothing but trouble since she arrived—"

"Take her to the medical bay," the woman interrupted. "Have them treat her burns. Then put her on probation. We'll see what Commander Kane says about this."

# 16

Silence was a sound in and of itself, Ember decided. To a race who liked to congregate, it had to be specifically sought. She hadn't had much of it growing up, not with her neighbors sleeping just feet from her head and chickens clucking throughout the house. She'd grown up surrounded by the sounds of her father's snoring and her mother's whispers and quiet breakfast preparation as she slept.

That was what bothered her most about this place. The quiet. It was unnatural.

*As unnatural as a Roma girl melting a machine.*

She'd returned from the medical bay about an hour ago. The salve on her burned skin was already nearly gone, having taken most of the pain with it. Thankfully the burns were the worst on her exposed skin and she'd been wearing her jacket and trousers, so it wasn't as bad as it could have been. No, it wasn't the burns that bothered her.

It was the way everyone had looked at her afterward.

The officials must have explained that the machine was down, because the flickers were sent back to their quarters to await further instructions. A few still lingered in the corridor outside her room. Their looks of disgust and wariness told her they'd figured out that Ember was the one who'd broken the machine. Stefan was nowhere to be seen.

She hadn't done it on purpose. Had she? What would this mean for her escape plan?

A soft knock sounded at her door. "Enter," Ember called out.

Mar walked in, arms folded across her chest. "We need to talk."

Great. Ember wasn't in the mood for another lecture. "Make yourself comfortable."

"It was you, wasn't it? I know it was because you were the last one in there. You broke phase two with your *mind*."

"It wasn't intentional."

"Do you realize what you've done? That machine is how they place flickers, Ember. It analyzes our strengths and puts us in the right program. You just brought testing week to a screeching halt while they order a new machine from High Commander Kane's facility on Terantine. We'll be stuck here a few days longer, maybe even another week."

A week. She could find a cargo ship and pilot in that time, especially if they set the flickers free in the city again.

Mar got right in her face. "You don't look sorry at all."

"Mar," Ember began. "I don't know what happened. I certainly wasn't trying to slow you down—"

"No, listen to me. There's just one thing I want to know." Mar plopped herself into the chair opposite Ember, then a huge grin spread across her face. "How did you do it?"

"What?"

"No, really. It was brilliant. Did you start a fire in there or something? Because, honestly, I think it was the cleverest trick ever. I can't believe you pulled it off."

Now Ember was really confused. "You're not upset?"

"Why would I be upset? I don't want to be here any more than you do."

She certainly hadn't acted like it so far, but Ember wasn't about to disagree. "So you don't like being a flicker."

"Oh, I don't mind that part. It's just the whole being-used-by-the-Empire thing I don't want. Sure it would be nice to be the first Olvenack to pass. I'm just not so sure about what comes after training." Mar examined her nails. "Nobody ever talks about that."

Ember sat straight up now, not bothering to hide her excitement. "So you want to escape too."

"Escape?" She snorted. "Nobody escapes an Empire station. That would be suicide."

Ember sat back. "Oh."

"The other flickers are so mad at you right now," Mar said with a chuckle. "Be sure to watch your back next time you go to the cafeteria. Eris went bright purple when she heard what you did. You'd think you melted her family instead of a stupid machine."

"Is Stefan angry?" Ember asked.

Mar's smile froze, then she turned on Ember, her expression guarded. "Stefan? Why do you ask?"

"Forget it."

Mar's eyes were boring into her now. "You think he's yours now because he bought you a drink on the rec deck, huh?"

Resentment sprang up inside Ember, and she wanted to tell Mar about the moments they'd shared—about Empyrean and the music and his grandmother's vision. But it didn't matter. Mar was right—he wasn't hers. She needed to get him off her mind before she accidentally fulfilled something she shouldn't.

"I've loved Stefan for years," Mar said, staring at the ground. "I know. I shouldn't have fallen for the guy every other girl wanted, and I only saw him occasionally when I trained at the station. But last year we finally became friends. He finally *saw* me." She glared at Ember. "And then you came. Now he looks right through me like I'm not even there. And you—he looks like he's never seen a woman before when he looks at you."

Now Ember didn't know what to say. A mixture of giddiness and dread fought for dominance within her. "I think you're seeing things."

"Then you're not paying attention." Mar stood and headed for the door. "Well, if you're going to escape, I guess you have a few extra days to do it now. I'll see you at dinner. Or not."

Ember stared out the window, her legs crossed on her bed as Mar exited. Then the room was quiet once again. The familiar *whoosh* of the closing door didn't sound, however.

"Close door," Ember muttered.

"I don't think so," a deep voice said.

Ember turned to find Talon standing in the doorway with several guards. She motioned for them to enter, and they filled the room in seconds, surrounding Ember where she sat on her bed, weapons raised.

Alarmed, Ember raised her arms in surrender. Had Kane decided to incarcerate her after all?

Talon followed the guards in, then stepped aside to reveal someone behind her.

Ember nearly collapsed in shock. "Ambrose?"

The smuggler stood there, for once looking a bit uncertain. "What is it you need again?"

"Confirmation," Talon told him. "Is this her?"

"Yep, that's her."

Ember couldn't breathe. A huge weight gripped her chest as the reality of it all crashed into her mind.

Ambrose had betrayed her. He wasn't on his way to Earth at all. Dai's medicine would never be delivered.

"Why?" Ember burst out. "How could you?"

Ambrose smirked. "You never saw it, did you, gypsy girl?"

Ember didn't play his game. She just glared at him, waiting.

"I'm a seeker, all right?" He shrugged. "When tourists returned from your market raving about the girl who told the future, I decided to check it out and pose as a smuggler—waited until I was certain before sending the tip to High Commander Kane."

He'd turned her in. Twice. This man was the reason Ember was here, hundreds of light years away from Dai and her home. She had no medicine to send home now and no money to buy more. Even if she managed to escape, no cargo pilot would smuggle her out for free.

Her hands curled into fists, and before she knew what had happened, she had launched herself at the man.

"Whoa there," Talon said, her long fingers grabbing Ember's collar and yanking her back before she could make contact. Ember fought to free herself from the woman's iron grip, but it was no use. "You may leave now, seeker."

The traitor tipped an imaginary hat and shot Ember an amused smile as he left. How much had he been paid to turn her in? A few credits? Hundreds? He'd gotten more than two hundred from her on top of that, and he'd probably resold Dai's medicine by now.

"Illegal shipping transaction," Talon said. "Not exactly what I thought I'd be arresting you for, but effective nonetheless. Say good-bye to your luxury quarters." Within seconds, Talon had Ember's arms locked together in front of her again. Her burned skin rubbed painfully against the metal clasps. Talon shoved her toward the door.

Ember couldn't sleep. They'd put her in a solitary cell, but she wasn't really alone. The tiny, cramped room was lined with glass to prevent privacy. The toilet and sink were a hard, unforgiving metal, and the bed was a cold steel covered with a thin mattress that may as well have not been there at all. They hadn't even given her a pillow.

But the cold metal was the perfect metaphor for the past three days on this station—hard, impersonal, and unbending. Devoid of any warmth whatsoever.

The true reason she couldn't sleep, though, was that her mind kept running through the events of the day.

She slumped down onto her bed again, tired of thinking. She didn't belong here. Her people at home didn't like her much, but at least they didn't hate her. There was just a wariness there, a lack of understanding. They'd believed what Babik and his father said about her. He had called Ember a killer, told them she was the reason his two friends were dead.

He was right.

From the perspective of her people, Babik's unrelenting determination to marry her wasn't all that unusual. Several other girls had been kidnapped and forced to marry their kidnappers, and none of them had killed anybody. In fact, most of the other Roma would have been relieved to have Ember claimed at last, no matter how it was done.

Except Babik's plan had gone horribly wrong. Ember hadn't meant to reach out to the intruders' inner light as she'd struggled against them. She definitely hadn't tried to lash out at them. She'd simply *pulled* and the light had followed. Babik's friends had fallen to the floor immediately, never to move again.

The details were fuzzy. Two bodies on the floor. Babik's terrified face staring at her as if she were a monster. Her screams. Babik running, then coming back to try one final time . . . or so she'd thought.

If Ember had only listened with her ears, she would have heard her mother's soft voice and realized it wasn't Babik returning. But she hadn't. Now in full-blown fight-or-flight mode, her body was too full of adrenaline to register identities. All she knew was that she had to stop the light from coming any closer.

And she had.

She could still see it nearly three years later—her mother's body on the floor, leg askew beneath the divider cloth. Her mother's expression of shock frozen forever in her mind. Her father's cry when he awoke and saw Ember hunched over his wife's twisted form.

How he'd looked at her . . . and then refused to meet her gaze for weeks afterward.

"I'm so sorry," she whispered. "It's my fault."

She fell asleep reliving the memory over and over again in utter and complete silence.

Hours later, a soft click penetrated her dreams.

Ember's eyes slid open and scanned her cell. She was alone. She listened for a moment, then allowed herself to drift away again.

Hands closed around her throat.

# 17

She tried to cry out, but only a tiny squeak escaped. She grabbed her attacker's hairy arm and tried rolling away, but he only tightened his grip. She kicked and thrashed and pulled on his arms, but the man simply grunted and held her tight.

Tiny white lights danced in front of Ember's vision. The beginning of the end. She gathered her strength and bucked her hips upward, twisting toward the wall.

It pulled the man off his feet, and he fell onto the bed on top of her. His hands loosened and he caught himself on one extended elbow. That precious quarter of a second was all she needed. She brought up her knee up and clocked the man's head. He gasped and released her throat.

*Babik. He's come for me again.*

She thrashed, the blanket tangling around her legs, and finally found the oxygen to scream. Just as her shriek escaped, a powerful blow struck her cheek. The lights danced in her vision again, this time lined with tiny red stars.

The hands found her neck again and squeezed.

Her heart slammed into her rib cage, threatening to fight its way free. She felt her lungs strain for air, her brain slipping into a darkness far greater than that of her cell. He wasn't here to claim her.

He was trying to kill her.

Ember flailed and thrashed with one last attempt at freedom, but her arms were too weak to make an impact. Her attacker seemed to sense it and tightened his grip even more. She had seconds left—if that.

She'd promised never to do it again. But now she was about to die.

Reaching out with her mind, she sensed a faint glow within her attacker and plunged her hand inside, ignoring the memories that pulsed around her.

Then she took hold of the light and *yanked* with everything she was worth.

The man's hands went limp, and he collapsed on top of her, his head dropping against her shoulder, his weight crushing her.

With a mighty heave, Ember shoved him off. He slid down and hit the ground with a heavy *thud*.

The room spun around her and small starlike lights popped through her vision when she sat up. So quiet. If not for the excruciating pain in her throat and the dark mound on the floor, she could almost believe she'd had an intense, terrible nightmare.

The trembling began at her feet and worked its way upward. Then her entire being was shivering, and she fell to her knees beside the bed, gasping for precious air through her damaged windpipe. She could still feel his hands on her throat. When some tiny shreds of her courage returned, she reached down to poke his shoulder.

Still as stone.

She reached out and felt for his light, trying to form a connection again, but there was nothing. *Nothing*. She had done it again.

Voices whispered softly in the hallway, and several figures appeared in the dim hallway light. Ember scrambled to the other corner of her cell, as far away from the body as she could get. As they approached, the cell light clicked on overhead and flooded her senses with painful brightness.

The door clicked open—the same sound she'd heard when the attacker came in—and two guards entered, their stunners aimed at Ember as Commander Kane stepped through with a grim smile. The guards examined the body on the floor with round eyes.

"I must say," Kane began. "I didn't think you'd surprise me. Well done."

Still breathing hard, Ember registered his words in a haze of confusion. She glared at the commander and at the body on the floor. The assassin's eyes were still wide open. He didn't look very intimidating at the moment—clean-shaven, younger than she'd expected. Early thirties, perhaps.

A guard knelt beside the body and felt for a pulse, then he turned to Kane. "Dead, sir."

Kane sent the body a pitying look. "Well, Frank. I suppose your bragging has come to an abrupt end."

"You sent him," Ember managed.

"You've officially passed the third phase, gypsy girl. You'll now move on to combat training on the Lennai'i."

His words finally slammed into her consciousness. "That was phase three? An *assassin?*"

"All the flickers had the same test." He watched her unblinkingly. "We initiated the next phase early, but I didn't anticipate that your test results would be so interesting. I'm still trying to make sense of it. You didn't even touch the man."

*All the flickers* had been attacked tonight. *Mar. Stefan.* Were they all right?

Kane had watched the whole thing on the security feed. If she hadn't fought back, Kane would have witnessed her death on screen.

"There's only one explanation, you know," Kane said thoughtfully, and Ember realized he was talking to himself. Kane turned to the guards. "All of you, out. Leave the body."

They hesitated a brief second before obeying, obviously concerned about leaving the commander locked in a cell with a killer. But they must have known better than to argue because they finally retreated, locking the door behind them and disappearing down the hallway.

The cell was quiet now. Ember couldn't take her eyes off the body at her feet. The guards could have at least taken it with them. The man looked much less threatening now. He wore a black jumpsuit, and his hair was neatly combed. Had he felt it necessary to style his hair before murdering her? Had it occurred to him that it might be the last time he did?

Kane ignored the assassin's still form and began to pace the room. "It was obvious from that first day that you were a flicker. It never occurred to me that you could be something else as well. Something I haven't seen in almost a quarter century. A *flare*."

She finally lifted her gaze. "A flare?"

"There's only been one other, and he's long since retired. I should have seen it. Of course the machine wouldn't work on you. It wasn't made to handle the intensity of your gift."

She shook her head slowly, not understanding.

"A flare has the power to not only read the inner light but actually grab hold of it, manipulate it. Even extinguish it, if they wish."

*Extinguish.* A terrible word for such an awful thing, and yet he'd described it perfectly. That was exactly what she'd done—ripped the soul out of another human being.

She had ended someone's life with a single thought.

*Stars. I don't want this. Why did you give it to me?*

He stopped pacing and tapped his chin thoughtfully. "Flares don't come out of nowhere, which means you must have an intriguing ancestry. I'll have to send a squad to investigate that gypsy village of yours. Flickers are useful, but they don't win battles. Flares, however, can win entire wars alone."

His words sank in, and suddenly Ember felt sick. She straightened, still trembling from shock. "I will never do that again. Not for you, not for anyone. I'm no weapon to be used as you see fit."

"Not yet, but I will make you into something powerful. They'll kneel at your feet before I'm done. The emperor will hear of this when he wakes."

"No. I won't do it." Horror crept up her spine, paralyzing her. "You will send me home and leave my people alone. We're peaceful, and I—I'm the only one with this gift. I'd rather die than be a weapon in your hands."

"That's exactly what the other flare said at first. He eventually saw the wisdom in my plan, and so will you. And your village will be tested for their own protection. Your kind are like pests. If you find one, there are usually more hidden somewhere."

Anger had taken hold of her thoughts now, and she felt herself reaching out to his inner light. She felt it pulsing just out of reach. He was angry too. She felt along the edges of his shield, wishing desperately that she could—

She pulled away, shuddering. There would be no more death. This horrible man deserved it, but she wouldn't become what he wanted. Not even if it meant ending him.

He nodded, seeming to see her battle. Then he headed for the door. One swipe of his wristband and the door clicked open. "Oh, and I'd be careful about revealing your gift to anyone else. Your secret is a dangerous one. Your guards are specially trained to deal with flickers, and they'll know if you try to read them. You'll be stunned before you know what—"

Ember lunged for the open door, cutting him off.

She had intended to shove him aside with her shoulder, but he whirled out of the way, recovering quickly. As she began to ease through the door's narrow opening toward freedom, he reached out and grabbed her head, then slammed it against the doorframe.

Pain exploded in her skull. Her legs buckled and she nearly hit the floor, but fought to remain on her feet. The doorway blurred in her vision. She reached out for it, desperate to escape.

Kane was a dark mass now. He drew closer, looming over her. "A gypsy girl attacking a High Commander with thirty-one years of combat experience. Too bad I turned the security feed off. It would have been great entertainment for later."

The dark blur shoved her backward. Ember wasn't prepared for it. She stumbled and collapsed on the ground. Her vision was finally beginning to sharpen as Kane pulled the door closed behind him and the lock clicked.

"Consider yourself fortunate," he said. "Anyone else would be serving a prison sentence for trying to smuggle something off a military station. But I'm submitting a pardon for you and taking you on as an assistant instead. The other flickers will be incredibly jealous." He turned and called out over his shoulder. "I hope you'll find our combat training ship, the Lennai'i, more suitable to your taste."

Ember stood, listening to his footsteps fade. Then she released an angry yell. She kicked the sink protruding from the wall over and over until a small dent appeared, then fell onto her bed and screamed into the mattress. She was tired of being manipulated, forced against her will, examined like a scientific specimen.

In her struggle to get home, she'd just made everything a hundred times worse.

They would descend on her village next. They'd test everyone. That meant they would plunge needles into the people she loved, prodding and invading. Perhaps even stealing them away for tests on a ship. Would there be anything left of her village when they were through?

And Dai. Would they find him and take him to a hospital?

They would test his blood with the others and find a DNA match. It wouldn't be long before they found an Empire connection.

She thought back to the article, feeling her stomach sink. It had featured a man named Mario Nicholas. Her father's name was Nicholae. He'd wandered into their village in his late twenties and told everyone he was studying Roma culture. It wasn't long before he fell in love with her mother and decided to stay—or so he'd told her. Was there more to it? Had the village simply served as a convenient hiding place from the Empire?

Her heart ached as she thought back to their last conversation. She could see it now. He'd been trying to tell her the truth about her gift without scaring her. He'd tried to convince her to marry, to join the protection of a man's house. To be hidden away from the claws of the Empire as a boria. Was it a father's concern or something more?

All his warnings about avoiding officers and hiding her gift. His prediction about his impending death. It all suddenly clicked, and her entire perspective shifted.

*You don't know that,* she had protested.

*I do, my Ember.*

Maybe it was true. Perhaps he'd read his own future in his daughter's inner light.

And now she was to take his place at Kane's side.

Ember was now indispensable. She'd be under the highest security, watched every moment day and night. And if she somehow managed to make it home, Kane knew exactly where to find her.

Her escape would have to be quick and unexpected. It wasn't about Ember and Dai anymore—it was the entire village. It was her way of life that was at risk now. The moment an opportunity presented itself, Ember would be gone. She'd go home, fetch her father, warn her people, and escape to the farthest reaches of the realm—so far the Empire would never find them again.

# 18

Three days later, Ember sat at the desk of her new quarters and glared at the desk screen in front of her.

ACCESS DENIED

She closed the error screen and tapped the word *news* again. The error message returned.

"You could at least tell me what's going on," she muttered to the screen.

They'd transported her to the Lennai'i under extremely high security, belting her arms to her chest and even blindfolding her. The gesture was amusing. She could ignore Kane's warning and read her guards if she decided to.

A full day of travel, then two days locked in her quarters. She hadn't spoken to anyone since her arrival. Occasionally she heard a guard cough or sneeze outside her door, but they ignored her questions. Meal trays appeared through a hatch four times a day. When she thanked whoever brought them, nobody replied.

"Come on," Ember grumbled at the desk-screen error message. Even if there was no news of Earth, she had to know what was going on with the other flickers. Were Mar and Stefan safe?

She felt physically ill when she thought of the assassin in her cell. She'd barely survived, and she had a special ability they didn't.

Her quarters were irritatingly luxurious, a stark contrast to her cell and consisting of three rooms—a sitting room, an office, and a bedroom. It all felt like such a waste. Lennai'i wasn't its own planet like the station but rather a massive triangular ship with an opening in the center. Whereas the station's walls and floor had been a bright white, this ship was all silver and black, sleek and modern. Ember hated every inch of it.

Her solitude gave her plenty of time to think, but that was the last thing she wanted to do right now.

Ember sighed and gave up on the desk screen, eyeing the food tray that had arrived minutes before. She always left the fork and the meat untouched, but the rest was decent enough, much better than the station's vegetable glob. She lifted the bowl of yellow sauce to her mouth and took a sip. It tasted like apples. She finished it off and glared at the tiny grayish-brown square in the corner. If that was dessert, it didn't look very appetizing.

When she heard movement at the hatch, she gave her tray one last look, then shoved it through. "Thank you."

"You're welcome," a female voice said, taking the tray.

Ember recognized her immediately as one of the guards who had escorted her here—Amai, a woman ten years older than Ember but who looked to have lived four lifetimes. She had never been rough with Ember, just distant and quiet. These were the first words the woman had spoken in her presence.

Ember was so surprised to receive an answer she stumbled over her next words. "When does Commander Kane get here?"

"He just arrived this morning," Amai said, still holding the hatch open. "He's coming to see you any minute. His security team just informed me."

Ember's surprise at the woman's detailed answer was overcome by dread mixed with a tinge of relief. Kane was already here. That meant whatever he'd done to her village was finished. Did he have Dai? Was everyone else safe?

The hatch was still open. "You're one of the more powerful flickers, aren't you?" Amai asked in a low voice. "You must be for the commander to be so interested in you."

So Kane hadn't told them what she really was. Of course he'd want to keep his new weapon a secret.

"He thinks I'm something I'm not," Ember finally said.

"I see." The woman paused. "Now that the commander has arrived, they're going to reassign us. I know this is a little unorthodox, but I was wondering if you could do a reading for me before he gets here."

Ember had resisted using her gift since that night in her cell. *Curse* was a better word. The stars obviously hated her. The last thing she wanted was to pretend like she was a good person.

It was just that killing that man had been so easy.

"I'd rather not," Ember said. "I'm not exactly safe to be around right now."

"I, uh—my daughter is missing," the guard rushed on. "I was hoping you could tell me what happened."

Ember closed her eyes, guilt flooding her. "That's not how it works. I can't read her future. Only yours."

"If you'll try, maybe I can help you."

Ember sat back against the door. "Help me? As in get me out of here?"

"Maybe. No promises."

She sighed. Then she hesitantly, carefully reached for the woman's light. It met her with an eagerness she hadn't experienced before. If the woman had a mental shield, she was obviously experienced enough to remove it on demand.

Ember scanned through the woman's memories. She did have a daughter, but the girl was a teenager. She pushed forward to the less-sure edges of the light, then pulled back with a gasp.

"Your daughter isn't missing," Ember said, not bothering to

hide the accusation in her voice. "She went off to join the Union. You already knew that." The full effect of what she'd seen hit her hard. "You're with the Union too."

"Keep your voice down," Amai whispered. "They monitor you day and night. If you look up, you'll see the cameras."

Ember had noticed them within minutes of her arrival. "Why did you lie to me?"

"They asked me to investigate a rumor. A powerful flicker, someone who broke a testing machine. It has to be you."

"So you're sizing up the competition."

"No, we're making you an offer. We want you to join us."

Ember groaned. "And leave one side to fight for another? How many times do I have to tell you people? I don't want to be involved in your war. I'm not a weapon, and I'm tired of being used. I just want to get home."

"To Earth. Yes, we know where you're from, and we know about your village. Commander Kane recently sent a testing team in. Last I heard they were still there. We can't keep everyone safe, but we can retrieve your immediate family. Assuming you agree to join us."

*Dai.*

Excitement rose in Ember's chest, but she stamped it down. "And what would be expected of me?"

"We can't get you out yet. We'll need you to be a special agent for a while, gathering intelligence and trying to minimize damage to our forces until we can send a unit in to get you. It will probably be a few more days. After that, your specific role will be determined by the Daughter herself."

"The Daughter? Who's that?"

"We'll answer all your questions when we can." She cut off quickly, then rushed on. "Kane is almost here. Do you agree or not?"

Joining the Union couldn't possibly be worse than working

for the Empire. That much was clear. And if Kane's team hadn't found Dai yet, the Union could whisk him away to safety.

Dread formed in her belly at the lack of information, but she ignored it for now. They were offering her everything she wanted. "I'll join you if you get my dai—I mean my father—somewhere safe. His name is Nicholae. Oh, and my friend Bianca and her son. And husband."

"I was told immediate family only."

"Those are my terms. It's only four people." She wasn't sure how Bianca would feel about being torn from her home, but Ember couldn't risk her friend's safety, especially when she was so vulnerable. Ember owed her that much.

Footsteps and voices sounded in the corridor.

"I'll do what I can." The hatch snapped closed.

Kane's voice echoed outside her door. He had seen Amai looking through the hatch. They exchanged low voices for a moment.

"You will report to Commander Furough's office for disciplinary action immediately," he finally said.

"Yes, sir."

A click sounded in the door and it slid open. Kane entered alone with a broad grin, as if completely unconcerned about her ability. He strode to the seating area and plopped down into an overstuffed chair.

"Sit," he said. "I've spoken with your village chief, and he had a very interesting story to tell about you. It seems my theory is correct about your gift."

As always, she folded her arms and remained standing. "Gift? You imply that it was given to me, yet you deny the source. The stars didn't mean for it to be used in this way. I'm not a killer."

"I assure you, if you cross me in any way, your village will pay for it. That's exactly 462 deaths on your head. That's not including the three gypsy lives you took a few years ago. I suppose you could say the rest are depending on you for their lives now."

She flinched, her earlier dread weighing heavy in her stomach. He knew everything.

If she escaped with the Union, there was a chance Dai and Bianca would be okay. But was it worth the deaths of everyone else to accomplish it? There was no way the Union would agree to rescue the entire village. It was too dangerous.

Ember felt the hands closing around her throat again.

"Your defiance up till now has been admirable. Foolish, but still admirable. Things are about to change. As my special assistant, you'll be doing a great service for the emperor. The entire realm, really. Our enemies have done terrible things, committed atrocities you can't imagine. They've destroyed entire worlds full of people without a second glance."

The *Union* had destroyed worlds? Of course Kane would see it that way. "Have they murdered a village full of innocent settlers just to make a point?"

"This isn't about avoiding death, gypsy girl. It's about choosing who lives—the peaceful cities of our Empire or a group of coldhearted killers."

"I don't see why there has to be a choice at all."

His smile wavered just a bit, then he stood. "Whether you agree with my methods or not, your training begins tomorrow. When you're ready, we'll give the emperor a demonstration of your power. If you refuse to cooperate, your village and everyone in it will be burned to the ground. But don't worry too much. You'll still have somewhere else to go." A dark glint entered his eyes.

His words felt like acid to her ears. "That will never happen."

"We'll see."

He made his way to the door. It opened to reveal several anxious guards standing outside. Amai wasn't there.

The door clicked closed behind him, and Ember was alone once again.

# 19

Ember spent the rest of the day pacing, and she couldn't sleep that night. Whenever she closed her eyes, she saw home. Soldiers running about, shooting people down and setting buildings on fire. Kane standing there laughing.

Every time a noise outside her door roused her, she sat up and listened for Amai's voice. Ember had to talk to the woman, tell her she'd changed her mind. Either they agreed to protect the entire village or she wouldn't cooperate.

To her disappointment, Amai never returned.

A tray of breakfast was shoved through the hatch the next morning, but Ember didn't eat anything. She sat at the desk, trying every possible combination of passwords and terms. She tried taking a shower, but the hot water just reminded her how far she was from home. Ember even tried talking to the guard outside, but he refused to respond. She touched his inner light and pulled back in disappointment. His defenses were rock hard.

The door opened without warning. Ember stood to face two guards.

"We're to take you to Commander Kane's office," the woman

said. It wasn't Amai. The guard's companion held out the clamps expectantly.

With a sigh, Ember allowed him to lock them over her wrists. Then they set off.

The corridors looked much the same as in the station—one dizzying hallway after another. The Empire liked things uniform and dreadfully dull, it seemed. They turned several corners, rode a lift upward, and then emerged into a much emptier corridor. They took her directly to the last door, where the woman swiped her wristband and let them in.

Commander Kane sat at a conference table, another man sitting to his right. Ember blinked and stumbled, nearly tripping over her own feet.

Stefan?

He gave her a grim smile, but there was nothing happy in his expression. Stefan seemed resigned more than anything. His eye was discolored as if he'd recently had a black eye, and he moved carefully.

But he was *alive.*

"Gypsy girl," Kane said, waving the guards away. "We were just talking about you. Come sit down."

Ember's gaze hadn't left Stefan. She watched him for any indication of what was happening, but he refused to meet her gaze.

"The emperor was concerned about your loyalties, girl," Kane said. "He requested that I ensure you're to be trusted since you'll be serving so closely with some of his highest officers. There is only one way to be sure. I believe you two know each other."

Of course he knew that. There had to be plenty of footage of their evenings together. The Empire would have tracked everything. The only thing she didn't know was how much Kane had overheard.

Kane motioned to Stefan. "Please."

Stefan didn't hesitate. He gestured to the chair across from him. "This will be easier if you sit and relax."

"I don't understand. What's going on, Stefan?" Ember asked, her stomach dropping at his morose expression.

"I'm going to read you."

Ember shot a glare at the commander, who sat back, looking rather pleased with himself. Then she understood. Kane didn't care what Ember had chosen to do. All he wanted to know was whether she would really cooperate or not. Even if she committed to him now, she could still turn on him later. This way he would know for certain.

And who better to perform the reading than the one person Ember trusted? It was the perfect way to crush any remaining hope she still held.

"This isn't necessary," Ember said, scrambling for her fragile emotional shield once more. If Stefan told Kane she'd been making deals with the Union, it would be the end of the village. She had no doubt Kane would make good on his threats. All of them. She locked her eyes on Stefan. "You promised you would never read me without permission."

"If I promised that, I shouldn't have," he said. "Are you going to stand, then?"

Anger sparked inside her, and she strengthened her mental shield against him. How dare he betray her, set aside all they had shared? How had she allowed herself to trust this man? The way he stared at the ground, almost like she was a stranger . . .

Stefan's features relaxed for a full minute. Ember tried to sense his touch on her light, but she couldn't feel anything. Just a slight brush on her shield. Was it strong enough to keep him out? She found herself breathing hard, tensed as if ready to spring. She wondered if the door was locked or if she could make an escape right now. But, no, there would be guards outside.

Stefan's eyes finally focused and he settled his gaze on her. The emotions she read there were complicated. Warmth, a certain ache. Sadness.

And something else. He was giving her a warning look.

He turned to the commander, and then the expression was gone. "I saw her at your side, sir. She loves her people too much to abandon them. She'll align herself to your will on their behalf."

Kane nodded, not seeming surprised. "Thank you, Stefan. I'm pleased you made it to combat training. I'm sure your service here will greatly please your parents and the emperor, long may he live."

"I hope so, sir."

"Dismissed."

Stefan walked swiftly out, leaving her alone with the commander.

Ember stared after him.

"The highest families are the most loyal," the commander said. He clasped his hands together. "Now that we have that settled, it's time for a little test."

For some reason, Kane felt it necessary to move them to a large room with a window. He locked the door behind her, sending a chill down her back. She reached out and felt only a few dim lights, all several rooms away. Kane had cleared the surrounding hallways of any guards. So they wouldn't overhear, perhaps?

Ember's heart raced as she scanned the room, looking for anything that could be used as a weapon. A desk with a screen. Several chairs, most of which were too soft, even if she could throw them any significant distance. Several cupboards set into the opposite wall with keypads. Nothing unusual for an office.

"There now," Kane said, sitting at his desk. "Let's see where you are in your training. You will obey my every order with exactness and immediate obedience. Do you understand?"

She eyed the door, half hoping Stefan would break through and say it was all a lie. But she knew that wouldn't change anything. Stefan had just confirmed what she already knew—her destiny was at Kane's side.

Her insides twisted at the thought.

"I asked you a question."

"Yes, sir," she managed.

"Excellent. Now reach out with your mind and extend outward as far as possible. Feel your shipmates but push farther than that if you can. Tell me how many ships are around us and where they are."

She closed her eyes, but her body shook too much to focus. She took a deep breath and began to hum, and finally she began to relax. She convinced herself she was somewhere else, far from here. She was home and safe.

"Six," she finally said, not trying to hide her surprise. She'd never tried to read from any significant distance before. Yet the people in those ships may as well have been right in front of her. Their lights blended together a bit from here, but if she focused enough she could separate them. "Two in front and four behind. And we're all moving, traveling somewhere together."

"Good." He sounded almost giddy now. "Now look for one called the *Mandilyn.* Tell me about the captain."

She jumped from ship to ship, then finally settled on the farthest one, a fighter with a crew of thirty and several squads of soldiers. This vessel was meant for ground combat. Strange that they'd be so far from a planet.

"Captain Lois Vaughn," she said. "An older lady with forty-two years' experience in battle." A kind woman, a survivor. She'd joined the military after her son's death. So much war, so many lives saved and lost at this woman's hands.

Ember felt her tension give way to relief. The commander didn't mean to attack Ember, or he would have done it already. He was just helping her extend her reach, probe deeper and farther. She could handle—

"Now extinguish her."

Ember's eyes flew open, and her humming stopped. "What?"

"That's a direct order. Do it now."

Ember stared at him. Surely he hadn't just ordered her to *murder* the woman. "But, sir—"

"You didn't just say 'but,'" Kane snapped. "This is what comes of a woman with absolutely no prior military training. When I issue an order, the only appropriate response is 'Yes, sir.' Now, I'll say it one more time. Extinguish the woman you just described."

His words were a jumble in her frantic mind. She saw herself once more, standing next to this man in the window. Her mother's death had been a terrible, horrifying accident. That assassin had been self-defense. But this? This was murder. And this wasn't her, no matter what her future said.

She drew herself together and looked the commander in the eye. "No. I won't do it."

His response was unexpected. Rather than leaping up and beating her into submission, he sat quietly. "Very well," he said, almost sounding bored. Then he stabbed something on the desk screen. "Assistance needed in my office, please."

"Right away, sir," Talon's unmistakable voice said.

"Now where did I put that thing?" Kane muttered to himself, almost as if Ember wasn't even there. The commander stood and made his way to the cabinets on the far wall. He placed his hand on the security screen, then punched in a code. The door clicked open, and he retrieved a small black bundle as the office door slid open.

Talon stepped inside and saluted. "Sir."

Kane slammed the cabinet closed and handed Talon the bundle. "Place this on the gypsy girl's neck, just at the throat. This sensor goes right on the spine." He shook the object out, letting the circular material hang in his hands. A collar.

Ember stumbled backward as Talon took it. She whirled and leaped for the door, but Talon's fingers dug into her shoulder and dragged her back. Ember spun around and threw a punch at the taller woman, which Talon easily dodged. Ember dropped to the ground to break the woman's contact and sprinted forward, but the lock clicked before she got there. There was no manual unlock button, which meant Kane must be holding a remote of some kind.

She turned, looking for another exit she might have missed, just as something cold clamped onto her neck. The metal rested on her upper spine. Ember tore away just as Talon stepped backward. "Done, sir."

Kane was back at his desk, fingers flying across his screen as if Ember hadn't just tried to escape. "Now let's see if it's positioned properly." He tapped a button.

A jolt of fire shot down Ember's spine. She gasped and arched her back, stumbling backward against the locked door.

"It appears so. Talon, you are dismissed with a reminder as to the nature of your agreement."

"Discretion as always, Commander." Talon eyed Ember with a curious frown. "Would you like me to secure her for your safety, sir?"

"She's no threat now. You may go."

Talon saluted and strode toward the door, which opened to admit her. Ember moved to follow and was rewarded with another jolt. She watched the door slide shut in front of her as the pain receded.

"You've witnessed only the first setting, gypsy girl," Kane said. "There are more levels to explore if needed."

She lifted a reluctant hand, letting it hover over the device around her neck. It was soft like fabric, so it moved with her, but lay stiff against the skin of her neck. The moment her finger brushed against it, the collar gave her a little zap.

Kane's expression was one of forced patience. "The device can't be disabled, sliced, or dented. Even a single touch can result in dreadful pain, as you've just demonstrated. Try to remove it and you'll be dead in seconds. One of my last inventions before I was raised. I sold the technology to the emperor himself."

Gritting her teeth, Ember slowly turned to face him. "Torture, then? You're going to electrocute me until I obey like a good little dog?"

"Torture?" He chuckled. "I prefer the term 'training.' Or even better, conditioning. Eventually even the most resistant animals see their place and allow their masters to guide them. Now, let's start again. Find that captain and extinguish her." His finger hovered over a small device in his right hand.

Ember thought of the woman again, the captain who had sacrificed so much and served the Empire well. Then she straightened, steeling herself for another jolt. "Push your button, but I won't do it."

"Very well." He tapped his desk screen.

Pain like nothing she'd ever experienced penetrated her body. Her back arched, and she slammed onto the floor. Her ribs ached at the impact, but she barely noticed. The knife in her spine twisted deeper. The pain intensified until Ember thought she would lose the contents of her stomach. Just as she was about to release a scream, the pain ended.

She lay on the floor, shaking.

"The emperor paid good money for this technology," Kane continued. "Enough to buy a planet, maybe even two. He wanted to use it as an information extraction device for the captured Union prisoners, but that perspective is terribly limited. This is so much more effective." He was standing over her now.

The room was a blur, her breaths came in quick gasps, and her body was in deep shock.

"One elderly woman," the commander said. "She's frail and likely to die soon anyway. Do it now."

Ember wanted to weep, to scream, to lash out at this terrible man who wanted her to become something she wasn't. The thought of enduring that horrible pain again was unbearable.

But she wasn't the person she'd seen in that awful vision. She couldn't be what Stefan had described. Surely the stars would allow her a choice.

She reached out—not for the elderly captain but for Kane. She slipped past his defenses and grabbed hold of his light before he could stop her.

*Lazarus smiled and lifted a single finger, then pointed it at the largest enemy ship.*

*The lights in the windows flickered and died. The starboard thrusters went next. His fighters, seeing the massive ship's shields disabled, quickly swooped in to finish it off. Seconds later, a huge cloud of fire consumed the vessel.*

*He grinned again and pointed at the next ship.*

*The girl at his side flinched. He admired her slender form as she stood there, her dark eyes wide at the realization of what she had just done, her black hair falling forward into her face.*

The pain took hold of her again, and she found herself writhing on the floor. She could see Kane's still figure staring down at her. His face was bright red.

It lasted far longer than it had last time. The world was red-hot fire, burning through her cells one at a time. It lanced her like a million hot knives until the room no longer existed. The world was simply pain.

It ended abruptly.

Ember's body trembled. She forced her eyelids open, but her vision refused to focus. Her heart hammered so quickly she thought it would thump right out of her chest. Her cheeks were wet with hot tears.

"If you ever so much as brush my shield again," he said in a dangerous tone, "I will kill you and everyone else on that pitiful planet of yours. I've no use for a flare who refuses to cooperate. For the last time, you have five seconds to extinguish that pitiful excuse of a captain. Five, four, three . . ."

She reached out to the captain again, feeling the woman's life pulsing with an unusual brightness. The woman was training in her quarters, just like she did every day. She had no idea her right to live was being decided several miles away in a dim, cold office.

Ember tried to move her hands, but they refused to comply. She finally managed to lift one to her neck, although it shook so wildly she could barely control it.

"Two."

*I'm sorry, Dai. I wanted to help you, but I won't do this.*

"One."

Her fingers hovered over the collar as she gathered her courage. Then she let her fingers close around the fabric and pulled all at once.

There was only pain.

And then nothing.

# 20

The surface beneath her face was hard and cold.

Ember lifted her head and immediately shielded her eyes from the bright light. The square room glowed with a blinding whiteness—the walls, the floor, everything. Cool air circulated around her bare shoulders. Her jacket was gone.

Was this heaven? Or that white mountain place Stefan had shown her—Empyrean?

"I know you're awake," a woman's voice boomed overhead. She sounded too bored to be a celestial being.

Ember blinked to allow her eyes to adjust. A black rectangle floated on the wall in front of her. She sat up and then doubled over. Sharp, stabbing pains shot through her insides.

"It's just your singed nerves misfiring. They'll straighten out eventually," the voice said. It sounded familiar.

"Talon?" Ember asked as the memories came flooding back. Kane pushing a button. The ship captain. *The collar.*

She hesitantly reached up, afraid of what she would find. Her finger made contact with the collar for the briefest second, but it issued a painful warning. Kane had left it on.

"The commander asked me to take over your training," Talon

said. There was a hint of smugness in her tone. "Said it was time to cover the basics since you're new to all this. I was more than happy to oblige."

"I bet you were," Ember groaned, forcing herself to her feet. "How long was I out? And what is this place?"

"An observation room, and you've only been unconscious a couple of hours. Kane canceled my itinerary for today so I could sit here and watch you drool."

"Nice of him to send me to the medical bay. You know, make sure I was all right and all that."

"Don't take that tone with me. You're lucky to be alive. The commander didn't have to lift his finger off the trigger, you know."

Ember's insides ached like she'd swallowed acid. Tiny pains still shot through her hands and feet, but they were nothing compared to the all-encompassing fire she'd endured earlier. "If he thinks this collar will turn me into his little assassin, he's wrong. I won't do what he wants."

Talon snorted. "You don't get it, do you? This is so much bigger than you and your morals. Whoever it was he wanted you to kill will just die another way. A slower, more painful way. Resisting Commander Kane won't save anybody. It'll just make things worse for you and anybody you've ever known or loved."

Her voice went soft at the end. Ember stared at the black glass, wishing she could see the woman's face. She reached out to Talon's inner light, but, of course, it was heavily shielded. "Let me guess. You're a flicker. And you resisted at first too."

Talon made a sort of gurgling noise, then the hardness was back. "You're obviously fine now, so it's time to start. Fifty push-ups."

Ember hadn't done push-ups since childhood. She rolled her eyes and lowered herself carefully to her knees. Then she gasped as the pain gripped her again, her back arching with the force of it.

"Too slow," Talon droned. "Seventy-five."

That was how the next hour passed, although it felt far longer to Ember. Talon guided her through a circuit—push-ups, jacks, then sprinting from one end of the room to the other until she thought she'd collapse from dizziness. Then she'd do it all over again with Talon yelling *"Faster!"* Her arms and legs trembled, but Talon refused to allow her any rest. The moment she hesitated or moved too slowly, the pain returned.

At one point Ember hit the wall a little too hard from her run and ended up flat on her back. She stared at the ceiling for perhaps a quarter of a second before Talon hit the trigger, sending Ember writhing into a ball.

"Stand up," Talon ordered.

But Ember couldn't. The nerves in her legs were firing, screaming. Her feeble attempt to move didn't even register. The pain only intensified. She pawed at the collar at her throat, wishing for the sweet nothing of unconsciousness.

The pain stopped abruptly. Ember collapsed to the ground again, gulping for air. Her heart beat erratically for a moment before finally evening out.

"Don't *ever* mess with the collar." If Talon had been angry before, now she sounded deadly. Ember wondered whether the woman would storm in and begin pummeling her as she lay helpless. "The commander said to show you this if you tried that again."

The black window lit up. It flickered for a second, then an image formed. Ember was staring at her hometown. It was dusk there, the dark-orange sun sending dark shadows behind the walls. A few lazy tendrils of smoke climbed toward a dull-brown sky.

"His seekers have been testing residents for days without success, but Kane ordered them to stick around. If you advance in your training, everybody wins. The soldiers keep their distance. But if you knock yourself out again . . . "

A longer pause this time. Then the screen shifted to a little girl about six—Jaelle, her neighbor's daughter. Two soldiers stood behind the girl, their hands gripping her tiny shoulders. They motioned to the camera, and she threw a hesitant wave, but the expression on her face was one of terror.

Ember knew exactly what was running through the girl's mind. She was supposed to steer clear of gadje, and now two of them were holding the girl hostage, forcing her to act friendly to a machine when all she wanted to do was finish dinner with her family and sleep in her warm bed.

Ember's voice was flat. "If I resist, my people suffer for it."

"Well, technically she won't suffer. It'll be a quick, clean death. Her family will suffer, though, especially when they hear you could have stopped it."

Kane had already removed Ember from her home. Now he wanted to cut any remaining ties and any lingering hope. He didn't realize how effective that would be. If her kumpania didn't hate her already, this would definitely tip the scale. And if Ember did manage to escape and return, they'd kill her on sight.

She rose to her feet, her hands balling into fists to hide the trembling. She would cooperate for now, if only to buy herself and her people time. She wanted to scream at them to leave that place, to escape the soldiers forever. There was just one tiny light in the darkness of her situation here—the fact that they'd chosen a random child to execute. If they knew about Dai, they would have used him.

"I won't attempt suicide or unconsciousness again," Ember said. "Tell them to set her free."

"Excellent."

A pause, then the soldiers stepped back from the girl. She looked around, confused, and finally ran off.

*Go home, little one,* Ember wanted to call after her. *Hide from the soldiers. The streets aren't safe anymore.*

"I think you've learned an important lesson today, Ember

gypsy. You may return to your quarters. Tomorrow's schedule will be posted on your wall screen. I'll see you back here at 1900. But, remember, as far as everyone else on this ship is concerned, your collar is a necklace, a special gift from Commander Kane himself. One touch, even accidental, and that little cutie on Earth goes bye-bye."

~

The next several days flew by. Ember spent mornings training with the other new flickers. She recognized a couple of them as friends of Stefan, but Mar was distinctly absent. A part of her hoped Mar had passed and made it to a different ship.

Another part hoped Mar had somehow managed to make it home to her world without walls and orders and killings. Ember couldn't face the alternative.

Each day was the same. Three classes followed by physical-combat training, then the simulator. Ember hated every second.

But she hated her time with Talon after dinner even more. The woman seemed determined to squeeze every last ounce of resistance out of Ember, who found herself instinctively obeying even the slightest command.

She told herself it was all an act, that she would play along for now. But it was disturbing how efficiently Talon had broken her. The tasks Ember performed grew increasingly difficult, particularly after a hard day of training. Yet as the days wore on, Ember grew to automatically and immediately obey every order, almost as if her mind had been removed from the picture entirely.

When Talon felt Ember had had enough, she would dismiss her into the care of a guard who escorted her back to her quarters every night.

Stefan wasn't in her group. She hadn't seen him since he'd broken his promise.

By the end of the fourth day, Ember felt like she was on a

conveyor belt. Sit, listen, regurgitate facts. Analyze the enemy, name their current formation and intent. Stay six steps ahead. Face off with another student; try not to get hurt too badly. Use your fists, your feet, your head to inflict pain. The same hands that did laundry and cooked for her father gradually grew quicker and more deadly. The Ember she had once been began to shrivel inside her.

It wasn't until she walked into the medical bay on day five that she saw Stefan.

She had tweaked her wrist again in combat training, and her instructor had insisted she get it checked out on the medical deck. Her guard took up his usual place at the door, checking his wristband. Stefan was heading out as she walked in. When he saw her, his steps slowed. Stefan's swollen eye was nearly healed now, and he moved with more certainty. Whatever his injury was, it seemed to be healing.

Good. Now he could learn to be a killer too. It was what he wanted, after all.

"Ember," he whispered. "I need to talk to you."

He probably wanted to apologize for betraying her. Again. Although he claimed innocence, he had shown Kane her gift at the market and gotten her kidnapped, then broken his promise to her in order to please the commander. As nice as Stefan had once been, it was clear where he stood now—and where she stood in his view.

She pressed her lips together and walked right past him. She ignored the greeter's insistence that she sit and wait, and she headed straight for her usual room. It was empty. She swiped a cold pack from the chill box and sat in the chair.

Stefan followed her in and settled himself against the wall, arms folded. "Are you okay?"

"No," she snapped. "I'm not okay. And I didn't ask you to follow me."

He flinched at the coolness in her voice. "I need to explain."

"Was I a nice, comfy step for you on your way up the ladder? Glad I could do that much for you."

"It's not what you think, Ember. I said those things to protect you. And you're not exactly qualified to lecture me on keeping a promise."

"I don't know what you're talking about."

"Don't you?" He folded his arms. "Then answer this. I told you something in confidence, and the next day everyone knew about it."

She went still, trying to remember what they'd discussed that night. *His grandmother.* "I haven't told anyone."

"Then explain why my grandmother was arrested the next day."

Ember stared at him. "Well, it wasn't me. I went to bed after that, and the next morning they shipped me straight here."

"After you killed your attacker in phase three." He spat the words, each syllable like a knife to her chest.

Anger simmered inside her. What right did he have to accuse her? "You're here too. Are you telling me you didn't fight back?"

"Of course I fought back. It was a simple test of our reflexes. I took him down with a choke hold."

"You didn't kill him?"

"No." His voice was incredulous. "Ember, I should have warned you that would happen. I figured you knew, just like everyone else did. They send in fighters to rough us up a bit and see how you handle yourself. That's it."

Rough them up a bit? That couldn't be true. Her attacker had tried to choke the life out of her. If she hadn't killed that man first, Ember had no doubt she'd be dead.

Stefan leaned in closer. "You've changed, Ember. I thought I knew who you were, but now I'm not so sure. First you broke the machine, then you killed someone. And then my grandmother got arrested. Now you're Commander Kane's pet."

She bristled. "I am not *his* anything."

"Hey," a passing medic said. "What are you two doing in here?"

"Leaving," Ember muttered. She cradled her wrist in one hand, deciding it didn't hurt all that bad, and strode toward the door.

Stefan jumped up and extended his arm across the doorway to block her escape. "I'm not done. Hear me out."

"Listen to you accuse and insult me? No, thanks." She started to duck beneath his arm.

He held out his other hand to stop her. "Look, there's something you need to know," he said, lowering his voice. "I didn't actually read you."

She raised an eyebrow. "My shield worked, then?"

He snorted. "No, it was as flimsy as paper. You really need to work on your inner defenses. I'm saying I didn't actually see your future. I pretended to for Kane's sake, then told him what he wanted to hear."

Her anger fizzled a bit at this new revelation. "I was perfectly prepared to take care of myself."

"And defy one of the most powerful beings in the universe? Yeah, that would've turned out great for you. Do you realize the power that man holds? They say he may be the next emperor, long may he live. Commander Kane comes from one of the highest families in the Empire. He owns a *planet*."

"So I keep hearing," she muttered.

"I knew if you became useless to him, he'd dispose of you," he continued. "I thought this way I could buy you time. But Kane is watching you too closely. Besides, with your schedule and your secret training sessions—"

"How do you know about that?"

He paused, suddenly very interested in the cupboard across the room. "I've been keeping an eye on you. But now it's clear that you aren't who I thought you were. I shouldn't have covered for you." He blew out a frustrated breath. "There's too much at stake, too many people who depend on me. I don't know what I was thinking."

He lowered his arm to let her pass, but her mind was too busy processing his words.

"You lied to the commander," she said slowly. "For me."

"It was stupid."

She stepped forward and touched his arm. The moment she made contact, his attention snapped back to her, his eyes full of pain.

"I think deep down you know this is wrong," she whispered. "This—this connecting with people for the purpose of getting them killed."

He went rigid, but he didn't pull away from her hand. "I know it seems terrible, but not all flickers do that. Sometimes they need us for intelligence or interrogation."

Ember snorted. "Like that's any better."

She tried to brush past him, but he planted himself in the way. "Okay, you're right about one thing, Ember. There's another reason I lied to the commander. I still think you're the one in my grandmother's vision, and you can't fulfill anything if you fail your training here."

"I'm not here to validate some old woman's fantasies," she spat. "And maybe I'd rather be dead than become the Empire's weapon."

"But if you just wait—"

"I'm done waiting." She shoved past him and marched down the hallway, feeling the disapproving eyes of several medics and patients from down the hall.

He caught up and grabbed her good arm, turning her around roughly. "You don't have to do this alone." He paused. "Where did you get that necklace?" He reached up as if to stroke it.

"Don't touch it!" she hissed, spinning away from him.

He recoiled sharply. Surprise registered, then hurt. "Look, I don't know when I'll see you again. Just remember that I'm not the enemy here."

"I know you aren't."

"Then why do you look at me like I am?" He stepped forward and lowered his voice. "Is this really about what happened the other day, or is there something more? Because you've kept a wall up ever since you read my future on the day we met."

*Because you're a gadjo,* she thought. *Because the same stars that brought us together also gave me a curse. Because I'm afraid that kissing you means the stars are right about who I am and what I'm capable of.*

Ember didn't want to admit the deepest reason. She clung to the truth, keeping it close to her heart where it was safest.

*Because I hurt those I love, even when I don't mean to.*

"You're imagining things," she said, but her voice broke on the last syllable, and she swallowed hard and looked away.

He had her pinned against the wall now. Her hands trembled at how close he was. There were no medical workers, no hallways. Just Stefan and his intense, anxious eyes completely focused on her.

"You saw something disturbing in my future that day in the market, didn't you?" he said. "Something that scared you. At least tell me what it was before you go." He brought a hand up to brush her cheek. She unconsciously leaned into his touch, awed at how natural and warm his skin felt against hers.

"I can't," she whispered.

Stefan looked disappointed, but he didn't pull away. If anything, he moved closer, his finger brushing her cheek. "If escaping is still what you want, I'm sure you'll make it happen." She could feel his breath on her cheek now. His lips were just inches away. She wondered what it would feel like to—

"What do you think this is, the rec deck?" the medic from earlier said, tapping Stefan on the shoulder. "Get out of here now, before I call security."

Stefan straightened as Ember turned away, the realization of what she had almost done hitting her like a slap. Stefan's gaze was still locked on her, watching for a reaction.

The medic gave her a pointed look. "I'm not kidding. Leave." Then she muttered something about flickers thinking they owned the ship and continued on her way down the hall.

"I suppose we'd better go," Stefan said in a hoarse voice.

"Wait." She grabbed his arm before he could turn away. "If I found a way for both of us to escape, would you come?"

He cocked his head. "What?"

"If you could leave all this, would you? Could you go live on a peaceful planet with no advancement pins and orders?" She paused and lowered her voice even more. "Would you join the Union if you had the chance?"

His face fell. "I—I don't know. The Union isn't exactly the most peaceful place to go. They keep attacking planets, Ember. And I can't leave my grandmother in prison."

She blinked. There it was again. Kane had made the same accusation about the Union, but she'd assumed that was Empire propaganda. Surely the Union was protecting the innocent, not killing them.

Although they had searched her out. That could only mean they wanted to use her as much as Kane did. And Amai had lied to her at first.

Ember hadn't seen her since that conversation. Was the woman looking for Dai now to get him to safety, or was there something more sinister behind her offer? Did they have their eyes on Earth next?

Ember's life was such a mess. Every time she tried to protect someone, she made it worse. Now wasn't the time to be thinking about kissing. She had a village to save.

"This—this *thing*," she said, motioning to the space between them. "Whatever it is, it ends now. You were right. It's not just about us."

"Ember—"

"I'm sorry."

She strode away without giving him a second glance. She continued down the hall, and her guard leaped to his feet after her, but she ignored him and made her way to the lift, trying to swallow down the hot, sticky lump in her throat. The guard hurried inside and called out for deck eight. The corridor was empty behind them as the doors closed.

Stefan hadn't followed her.

## 21

When Ember arrived at the simulator, she found the entire class standing in the crowded entry area. Her instructor, a woman with white hair and a stern face, nodded to Ember. "Thirteen minutes late. Thank you for volunteering, Ember gypsy." She turned her attention back to the class. "Raise your hands and share your observations."

Still fuming from her encounter with Stefan, Ember made her way toward the simulator's black doors. She was angry at him for coming to the market, for being kind to her on the shuttle, for making her question how terrible the Empire really was.

But the worst part was how efficiently he'd destroyed her defenses in the medical bay. Kane and Talon had inflicted a terrible, consuming pain on her to chip away at her resistance. All it had taken for Stefan to crack her resolve was a single touch, an almost-kiss. Her cheek was still warm where he'd cupped it in his palm. Or maybe the heat in her cheeks was something else entirely.

She entered the simulator room, which was built to resemble a launchpad. Two small three-person shuttles sat across from each other. There was someone in one of them, she noticed, although she couldn't tell through the dark glass whether it was a man or woman. She stepped into the empty shuttle and plopped into her seat.

"Begin," the instructor said, her voice echoing through a speaker overhead.

The other flicker immediately attacked, but Ember wasn't in the mood for a fight just now. She swerved the shuttle aside as she reached out to make an inner connection, but a thick shield blocked her.

She tried to reach behind it, to grip it and move it aside, but it was no use. Who was the other flicker? This person's shield was nearly as strong as Commander Kane's.

"Fine," she snapped at the controls. "We'll do this another way."

Ember feinted toward the hull and then pulled up at the last second. She gave the other flicker's shield another tug. It held.

The other flicker didn't hesitate, sending a series of shots toward Ember's wing, nearly ripping it clean off. None of it was real, of course, but it still jerked Ember out of her thoughts.

"All right," she muttered. "Let's have some fun."

She began to hum. The sound began to soothe her, calming her nerves as she tried once again. This time the shield was slightly weaker. She pounded on it, then reached back and smashed into it when the shield momentarily flickered.

It was all Ember needed. She reached in, searching for the wispy future of her foe, then groaned. *Eris.* When had she arrived?

A quick comb of Eris's memories held the answer. Eris had been knocked out by her attacker, failing phase three. But her rich parents had stepped in and saved her, insisting the test was rigged against her because she was from a higher family. The officers had eventually relented and, in an effort to calm her parents, sent her to accelerated training here. She had just arrived this morning.

Eris seemed to sense that Ember's attention was elsewhere because she diverted all power to her weapons and began her final attack. Ember tried to weave and shoot back, but it was too late. The other wing went out immediately, followed by the rear, where her power core was situated. Her ship blew up in an instant. An angry beeping sounded from the controls beneath Ember's hands.

"You lose, gypsy," the instructor said from overhead. "Eris, nice work. I can tell you've been practicing."

By the time Ember emerged, Eris had already joined the group, grinning and seeming to enjoy the pats on the back.

"Never look at your opponent's past," the instructor snapped at Ember. "Never. It will only distract you. Always look to the future and stay there."

"Right," Ember said, frowning. Did Stefan know Eris was here? Ember brushed her cheek where Stefan had touched her, then let her hand drop.

It didn't matter, because Stefan wasn't hers.

"Gypsy," the instructor said. "Here's your consolation question. Name three basic defensive maneuvers."

"For which ship?"

Her mouth twitched. "A freighter."

The rest of the class laughed. Ember resisted the urge to roll her eyes. A freighter had no chance in a battle. It was ridiculous to waste time on such things. "Most freighters have thrusters on three sides, so it's easy for them to move forward and backward. When faced with the enemy, they'll usually try putting distance between them. Or if they have the mass advantage, they'll thrust forward and collide with the offending ship on the ramming side. The third maneuver is usually dangerous because of the weight-distribution issue. Freighters carry their cargo in the back, with passengers and pilots positioned near the front. The rear thrusters can rotate downward and quickly propel the craft upward at a forty-five-degree angle, exposing the shielded side to the enemy and forcing them to move backward to prevent a collision."

"I didn't ask you to describe them. I asked what they are called."

Ember opened her mouth, then shut it again. She couldn't remember the terms.

"We've gone over this several times, gypsy."

"Point, Shield, and the Felding Loop, ma'am," Eris called out.

"Very good, Eris." The instructor gave Ember a pointed look. Irritation welled up inside Ember, but she bit her lip to keep from snapping back. Everyone else in the room was called by their name, not race. Why was she any different? And she'd answered the question in far greater detail than Eris. This type of thing was exactly why she'd quit school at age twelve.

"Cutter and Zain, you're up next."

When the class finally ended, Ember was first out the door, feeling her cheeks continue to heat up. Her guard strode behind her like a shadow as she headed to her next class. She was almost tempted to skip dinner and go straight to her quarters just so she could punch the life out of her pillow.

Someone grabbed her arm, pulling her to a halt in the crowded hallway. She yanked her arm free before realizing who it was. A guard, a woman with extremely short black hair.

"Amai?" Ember asked cautiously. The woman's hair was a different color, and she looked more somber than Ember remembered.

"I distracted your guard, but he'll find you eventually. We need to talk." She grabbed Ember's arm again and pulled her along behind her.

Ember yanked her arm free for the second time. "Well? Have you found Dai?"

"Yes." She strode down the corridor, forcing Ember to trot in order to catch up.

"Wait. You found him? Is he alive?"

"It's not safe to talk here. Follow me." Amai crossed the corridor and entered a set of doors labeled "Locker Room." The room was full of benches and metal doors built into the walls. Several people in various stages of undress glared at them as they walked past. Both men and women seemed to be using this room. Ember shivered at the thought.

Amai brought her all the way to the back, then opened a huge door and shoved Ember in. A wall of heat slammed into Ember, and she choked.

"The steam room," Amai explained. She motioned to where a small black hole in the ceiling glared back at them. "There's still a camera, but the steam did a number on it. Hasn't functioned in years. They just pretend it still works."

The heat was heavy on Ember's lungs. "Tell me he's still alive. Please."

"He's alive. Mostly. Although we're still trying to get your friend out. She's a little tougher since there's other family involved."

Relief and fear warred inside Ember. Dai was all right. There was still a chance. "Did you transport him to a hospital?"

"Of course not. The Empire swarms those kinds of places. But we aren't cavemen, you know. We have medics looking after him, and he's safe for now. It's just that we can't figure out what his illness is."

"Why not?"

Amai snorted. "Do you realize how hard it is to keep up on every illness for every species on every planet? And we don't have access to the Empire's mainframe right now. Anyway, we're doing what we can. He keeps asking for you when he's awake, which isn't often."

That was him, all right. Ember wiped her forehead with one arm, tempted to remove her jacket. She was already bathed in sweat. "And what did you tell him?"

"That I was coming to bring you back. It's a little sooner

than planned, but we've gotten word that this ship is mobilizing. We figured this would be a good time to send it to kingdom come."

A chill settled over Ember. "You're going to destroy the ship."

"No other way to get you out. It's not like we can waltz into the cargo bay and demand a shuttle. Your escape will require a huge distraction, and what better way than a series of system failures followed by a big explosion?"

"No," Ember said, shaking her head firmly. "Absolutely not. I will not agree to that. There are thousands of people on this ship."

"Thousands of *soldiers*, which means they're people who are trained and ready to kill innocents. And this isn't up for negotiation."

The other flickers, the workers. Commander Kane. *Stefan*. The medic who bandaged her up after classes. Her defensive-strategy instructor. The chefs who prepared her food, the soldiers who trained for war, her personal guard.

They would all die. It would be a major victory for the Union but at a terrible cost—and she would live her entire life knowing she could have stopped it. Was the Union really the more honorable side? Because from what she was seeing, it wasn't much different from the Empire. "I refuse to cooperate."

Amai sat forward, her dark eyes glittering dangerously. "Excuse me?"

"I'm not going if that's the plan."

"You're kidding me, right?" Amai snorted. "Tonight's fireworks have taken months to prepare. I have sixteen people working with me on it, plus the escape pilots. I had to pay that couple a ridiculous amount of money to take the risk."

Ember paused. "Months? But I thought you set all this up to get me out."

"Fine, I've been stationed here for a long time. It was lucky they sent you here, that's all. But none of that matters. You wanted to get back to your dad, and we're making that happen. We'll handle all the details."

Amai's answer was too quick. A feeling of dread began to swell inside of Ember. Something wasn't quite right.

Ember gritted her teeth. What choice did she have? Nobody else was offering her a way off the ship. The Union had Dai. That was all she needed to know. If she could get Dai and escape the Union somehow, they could be free of this war forever.

But.

She held thousands of lives in her hands right now. How could she exchange them for a trip to Earth? How did that make her any less evil than Commander Kane or the emperor? Where would it all end?

Stefan's face came to her mind. The way he'd examined her, reading her in a way that had nothing to do with light. The warmth in his eyes. She couldn't do it. No matter what his future held, she could never place him in the Union's hands. To them, he was just another dangerous flicker who needed to be destroyed.

*What is he to you, Ember?*

Amai sat back. "You're blushing now. There's a man, isn't there?"

Ember ignored the comment. "There has to be another way. Something more humane. Something that won't result in such catastrophic loss."

"Catastrophic loss? We're in the middle of a war here. If this ship is mobilizing, that means they've found our latest hidden base and they're going to destroy it, along with tens of thousands of innocent people. Now *that's* catastrophic loss." Amai got right in Ember's face. "We had a deal, and I've fulfilled my end of it. Now you get to fulfill yours."

"I am," Ember found herself saying. "I'll take the ship down myself."

Amai took a step backward, eyeing Ember suspiciously. "You'll do what?"

"Let me stay a little longer. I'll gather intelligence and try to prevent as many Union deaths as possible. If the ship gets too close, I'll shut it down my way." Her throat was dry, and sweat dripped down her forehead. Her insides felt like they were being baked. She couldn't wait to get out of this stiflingly hot room.

Amai's face was expressionless. "You'll have to be more specific."

Ember had no clue how to disable a ship, particularly one so large and heavily monitored. But she needed time. Desperately. "You'll just have to trust me. Tell the Union to prepare a shuttle for me when we arrive at the battle site. I'll wreak havoc here and disarm the ship so you can take your prisoners, then we'll be off."

Amai studied her for a long moment. "The Daughter isn't going to like this. I should hit you over the head right now and drag you out."

"Except you know I'd never help you that way. It's got to be on my terms."

"So it seems." Amai gave a heavy sigh. "But I'm keeping my team on call. If you fail, the ship goes up, and you with it."

"I won't fail. I swear it." She paused. "And tell my father I'll see him soon."

# 22

Ember woke to pounding on the wall outside her door. "Get up, gypsy," her guard called out. "You've been ordered to Commander Kane's office."

Before she knew what had happened, she was outside the commander's office door, bleary-eyed and confused. The guard ushered her in and closed the door behind her.

Kane didn't look tired at all. In fact, he looked almost giddy. His hair was gelled flat to his head, his uniform even more pristine than usual. He paced the floor with an uncharacteristic nervousness.

"There you are," he snapped. "Get into position."

"Sir?"

"By the window."

She made her way over and gasped. A small convoy of ships sat outside. No, a cluster of smaller Empire patrollers with a single passenger transport between them. They'd captured a ship during the night. It looked like a typical Empire shuttle, the type Ember had seen transporting tourists on Earth. It had no other distinguishing features.

She pressed her hands against the glass, immediately scanning the ship. Two passengers—a young couple.

Amai's words from last night came back. *I have sixteen people working with me, plus the escape pilots. I had to pay that couple a ridiculous amount of money to take the risk.*

With a sick feeling, Ember plunged into the woman's light. Then she pulled out, stunned.

It was them. These were the people charged with helping her escape.

They'd come to get her as planned, but she hadn't shown up. The couple had waited too long and gotten caught as she'd snoozed away in her bed. Amai hadn't been able to stop it. Or maybe she just hadn't bothered to try.

Now they sat in the cockpit, quietly discussing their options, hiding the terror they felt inside.

This was her fault.

She turned to the commander, trying desperately to smooth her face. "You need me to read them, sir?"

"My flicker team has already retrieved any intelligence of worth. The emperor is ready for his demonstration, gypsy girl. He wants to see what our proud flare is capable of. I trust Talon's training is now sufficient to the task."

*Stars.* The commander had chosen tonight for his demonstration, of all nights. He was going to make her kill the couple who had been hired to save her. Her stomach twisted so sharply she wondered if she could keep her dinner down. She took a step backward and ran into the window, the cold penetrating her back.

Something beeped on the commander's desk screen, and he suddenly looked nervous. "Stay against the window. You are not worthy to see his face." Then he hit the button and bowed, his voice sickeningly sweet. "Your Eminence. What a pleasure this is. How wonderful to see you looking so well."

"And you, Commander," a frail voice said. The emperor

himself. Ember longed to look over Kane's shoulder and catch a glimpse of the man who ruled the universe. His voice sounded surprisingly human, with an edge of pain. Much like her father did on his bad days. "Is my flare ready for action?"

"She is, High One. My men are hacking into the intruder ship's security feed now."

The window behind Ember buzzed and cackled with static electricity. She stumbled away to find its surface had changed. The glass shimmered, then changed to show a man and woman sitting in the cockpit of a cramped ship. They were even younger than Ember had realized, perhaps in their early twenties.

"The signal should reach you in a few seconds, Your Eminence."

"I see them. Proceed."

Kane turned to Ember, his voice strangely tight. "Take them out, flare. The woman first."

The man reached for his wife and pulled her closer to him. She was trembling as she stared out the window at the massive Empire carrier looming above them. Did she know? They couldn't hear or see the Empire ship's deliberations, but they must have had a sense of what was about to happen.

Ember bit her lip to keep herself from crying out. She couldn't do this. Not when that couple was here for her. It should have been her on the other side of that screen. She was the one who deserved to die.

Kane tapped the trigger, sending a zap down Ember's spine. She gasped but managed to remain on her feet. Before she had time to think about it, she reached easily into the woman's soul, feeling the warmth of the light within. The woman on the screen flinched as if she felt Ember's touch. Maybe she did.

"Remember my warning," Kane murmured. "My soldiers await instructions on Earth. I'll have them start with the young ones. That girl from last time, perhaps."

Ember shuffled through the woman's memories before she

could stop herself. Lillya, orphaned by a bloody Empire battle on Carene Two. She'd married her best friend and joined the Union just months before. The money from this job was supposed to buy them a new home.

Kane stepped closer, his mouth tight. She knew what his next words would be.

It was simple for everyone else. Two enemy soldiers, complete strangers, versus a child Ember had watched grow up from infancy. Anyone in their right mind would choose the child. But they didn't understand that Ember could see so much more than that. She *became* those she touched. For one brief moment there was no separation. And she pulled out just a little bit changed. The person she had just read was no longer a stranger.

Although, Talon had said her resistance wasn't saving anyone, that Kane would just kill his victims another way. Surely that was true in this case as well. If Ember failed to murder them, the fighters would just fire on the ship. Either way the couple wouldn't make it out alive. She knew it was true.

Why had the stars given her this curse? Why couldn't she live her life innocently, not holding any lives in her hands but her own?

Kane motioned to the soldier at the door. "Tell Captain Wymore on Earth to initiate."

"No," Ember said quickly. Her throat was so tight she could barely say the words. "I'll do it."

Ember forced her eyes to stay open as she grasped the woman's light. Ember would watch this. She owed the poor woman that much.

The couple stared into the camera, stiff and waiting, as if sensing what was about to happen.

*Stars, I'm sorry.*

With a massive sob, she closed her hand around the light.

And *yanked.*

The woman jerked and went limp, then hit the floor. Her husband released a wrenching cry and reached for her.

Ember's gaze dropped to the ground, and she folded her arms protectively around herself. Her connection had ended. She tentatively reached out to the man, but she didn't have to get close to feel his pain. His light pulsed brighter, hotter, angrier than any light she'd ever seen. It singed Ember even from a distance. She looked up to see his eyes boring into the screen, his expression twisted in agony and rage.

"The Daughter will rise again," he shouted through his sobs. "She will have her vengeance. Death to you all!"

She stared at the man in wonder. What strength he must have had to have everything taken from him and still confront his enemy. It was beautiful. Something stirred deep inside her, something she hadn't realized was there.

Ember lifted her hands, examining them. What had she become?

She had just killed someone. *Murdered* an innocent woman who meant her no harm. She had spent the past few years resisting Talpa's efforts to control her. She'd balked at the marriage offers she received and struggled to keep what little freedom she had. But today Ember had let Kane control her. He hadn't forced her into becoming his weapon—she had stepped into the role herself.

The same commander who had controlled her father for so long.

Kane lifted a stunner to Ember's head. His face was purple. "Take him now, or you and your filthy people die this instant."

She drew herself up to face him. "Then kill me. But I won't do this."

Ember expected him to kill her, almost hoped he would. But instead he slammed his fist onto the trigger in his other hand. The pain exploded into her consciousness, a bonfire burning her from the inside. It was ten times worse than before. A hundred times worse. Someone was screaming. She reached for the blackness but couldn't find it. There was only the pain.

"Kill that man and you'll have your relief." The voice seemed strangely disconnected.

She reached for the husband's light and found it again, still hot and angry. This time she let her hand hover. Talon's warning circled through her mind on repeat. The man would die anyway. She could save her people. So much pain.

Instead of pulling on the light, she slammed her fist into it.

The pain stopped.

She slid her eyes open in time to see the man collapse onto the control panel and go still.

Ember lay on the ground, shaking violently. No. That wasn't supposed to kill him.

"I'm pleased." The emperor's voice was still tinged with pain, but his pleasure seemed genuine. Ember wondered if Kane had muted the battle that had just taken place inside his office. "This is a welcome development. And you say the gypsy girl was homage from Earth?"

"Yes, Your Eminence."

"It would be nice to have more than one flare at our disposal. You've investigated the family line?"

"Of course. None of her family have the gene."

"Pity," the emperor said, his voice suddenly weary. "Carry on, then. I want the girl's abilities expanded to include more than one at a time. We won't win any wars if it takes ten minutes to kill two people."

Kane's face reddened, but he nodded. "Yes, High One. And my breeding-program proposal? I believe it wise to initiate it while the girl is still young. I will donate my planet, Arcadia, to the cause."

"No, no. Let's see how far we can push her first. Once the enemy is overcome, we'll discuss it again." The emperor's voice had faded to a whisper now. It seemed whatever strength he'd summoned for the conversation was gone. "You are dismissed."

"Thank you, Your Eminence."

The emperor must have clicked out, because Kane turned to Ember, who still lay on her back. She couldn't tear her eyes away from the screen that still displayed the man slumped over the ship's controls. She had been so determined, yet Kane had broken her. He had won.

Kane approached like a cat ready to pounce. He stopped in front of her. "You embarrassed me in front of the emperor."

The kick to her ribs came before she was ready for it, and she found herself doubled in a different kind of pain.

He glowered at her from above, his words slow and dangerous. "Do not hesitate like that ever again." Then he strode back to the desk and began messing with the screen once more. "Should have sent her straight there," he muttered to himself.

His words faded from Ember's mind as she continued to stare at the dead man's body on the screen. She reached out, wishing to feel his fire, to let his anger fuel her once again. Then she stifled a gasp. His light still glowed. It was faint, barely there.

Then the dead man's hand twitched.

The screen went dark, and all she could see were the stars outside once again.

# 23

Ember spent the day in her quarters. After she'd missed the first class, her guard had come in and tried to persuade her to come out, but Ember had told him off. She'd fully expected him to call in a reinforcement, but for the next few hours she heard him talking in a low voice outside her door. She didn't much care what they decided to do with her now.

After skipping breakfast and lunch, she barely noticed when a guard brought in a tray of dinner. A different guard this time, a woman. She shot Ember a pitiful look as she left.

Ember didn't want her pity. She didn't want their food, their fancy quarters. She just wanted to be home, caring for her father. She wanted to ask him the questions she'd never thought to ask. To the Roma he was an outsider. It didn't matter where exactly he'd come from, just that he hadn't been raised among them. Ember hadn't ever considered asking where he was born, who his parents were, where he had spent his childhood. Even when she found that horrible article about his military service, she had shoved the questions away. They just confirmed the strangeness, the other-ness, of her father's past life.

She'd give anything to go back now and ask him more. When had they discovered he was a flicker? Had he been raised on stations like Stefan? And the biggest question of all.

*Was he a flare too?*

She couldn't ask him now, but perhaps there was another way to find out.

When the hallway went quiet, Ember stepped into the corridor, noting with satisfaction that her guard had finally stepped away. Then she headed for the lift.

The recreation deck was much smaller here than on the station. In fact, it took up only a portion of the eleventh deck, and there were far fewer people. The music was just as loud, though; perhaps louder with less conversation to compete with. Couples grated against each other in the colorful lights. Ember grimaced at the assault to her senses.

She scanned the room and found the info screens imbedded in the wall on the opposite end. Only one faced away from the dance floor, its booth occupied by a couple in a passionate make-out session. Ember rolled her eyes. She'd wait a few minutes, then confront them.

Ember caught sight of Eris at the bar, holding a delicate glass with some kind of frothy pink concoction. Eris spotted her at the same time. But instead of glaring at Ember as she usually did, Eris's eyes flew open and she scrambled off her stool, spilling some of the drink onto her lap.

Then her companion turned around. Stefan eyed her for a moment, expressionless.

Ember realized some of the dancers had stopped and were now staring at her the same way. Some stumbled backward, giving her a wide berth, while others just glared.

She looked around, wondering if there was an officer behind her or something, but it seemed they were indeed staring at her. "What?" she snapped. Had word gotten out about this morning?

"Ember," Stefan called in a stiff voice, still sitting at the bar. "Let me buy you a drink."

Eris sent him a glowering look.

Half the room had noticed her now. Reeling, she found herself making her way toward the bar.

Stefan said something to the bartender, who promptly went to work filling a large round container, which began to emit thick white smoke. Then he slapped a cover on it and handed it to Stefan.

He passed it to Ember. "Here. You look like you need this."

She eyed it curiously. The bowl had a bubbly red liquid and some kind of plastic dome over the top.

"What *is* this?" she asked, examining the strange creation.

"The dome keeps the heat in. Just pull the lid off when you're ready."

Eris was staring, bug-eyed, at the strange drink. "Is that a steel mill? You're kidding me. She can't handle that."

"You'd be surprised." Stefan was glaring at his hands now. He seemed so formal, so aloof. The people on the dance floor had resumed their grating again, but Ember could still feel dozens of eyes boring into her back. Something was definitely wrong.

"Well?" Eris asked. "You going to stare at it or drink it?"

What she really wanted to do was pour it over the girl's head, but that seemed like a waste of perfectly good liquor. With a shrug, Ember snapped the dome off, releasing a plume of smoke, and brought the glass to her mouth. She heard some of the conversation around her die as she began to gulp it down.

Stefan had mentioned heat, but it wasn't figurative. An actual, physical heat surged down her throat and settled in her stomach, sending a shock wave through her bloodstream. She welcomed the pain, opening up to it.

"Check this out," someone said behind her, and his date shushed him. Stefan watched her wordlessly. His expression was just enough to get her through as the last few drops went down.

Then she decisively smacked the container against the clear counter.

A few people clapped, and Stefan's lips tugged upward. Eris's face registered shock, but she quickly turned back to her drink, feigning disinterest.

Ember glanced across the dance floor at the info screens. The couple was still there, hands roaming in improper places. If Talpa saw an unwed couple acting like that in public, they would be exiled on the spot. Or forced to marry. They probably wouldn't even notice if she used the screen behind them.

"Just out and about, then, gypsy?" Eris asked. "You aren't exactly a rec-deck girl. More like the hiding-in-the-shadows type."

"Just heading to the info screens." Her voice sounded hoarse. She coughed to clear her throat, suddenly wishing for a sip of water.

"I didn't take you for a gamer, either. I thought gypsies made their money dancing and singing. Among other things." Her gaze shifted to the couple across the room as well, and Ember caught the implication.

"Can I get you another drink, Ember?" Stefan cut in.

"No," a woman said, placing a hand on Ember's shoulder. "She's had enough for tonight."

Ember turned and blinked. Mar stood there, grinning.

She laughed at Ember's expression. "Well? You said we were gaming, right? Let's go." She took Ember's arm and pulled her toward the dance floor before Ember knew what was happening.

"You're here," Ember managed, her voice still a bit raspy.

"Well, you're a bright one, aren't you? Yep, I got here a few hours ago." She shrugged and released Ember's arm, still plowing through the dancing crowd. "I don't really want to be here, but I am. Security analyst, flicker division, at your service."

"I thought you failed phase three."

Mar snorted. "No, Eris failed. And miserably, from what I hear. I passed it, just not in the way they wanted."

"What do you mean?"

She grinned. "I waited by the door that night. When the guy came in, I whacked him over the head with a chair."

For the first time in days, Ember found herself smiling. "I wish I could have seen that."

The make-out couple must have seen them coming because they finally pushed to their feet and stepped out of the booth. They had difficulty walking they were so entangled, their hands in each other's pockets. Ember didn't have to guess where they were headed next.

Ember glanced back at the bar. Eris was desperately trying to capture Stefan's attention, but he was watching Ember out of the corner of his eye, an odd expression on his face.

"So," Mar said as she plopped herself into the chair the couple had just vacated. "What are you looking for? I'm assuming the gaming thing was just a ploy."

"I'll know it when I see it." Ember strode to the screen and hit it a little too hard. It lit up quickly. She settled into the other chair and began her search, swiping past the latest news. A missing freighter on an enemy planet, a disastrous-plague warning off the edge of the Gajon Galaxy. A new Empire station's construction announced in the twenty-third sector. Nothing about Earth or the Union. For as often as the commander mentioned his enemies, the lack of news seemed odd. How could there be no word of them when the Empire was constantly at war?

She switched to the search field and entered *Mario Nicholas.* Before she'd finished, two dozen articles sprang up, all with the tag *Flicker.* Her heart galloped in her chest as she clicked on the first one.

"You're looking up famous flickers?" Mar asked. Her grin had faded, and she stared at the screen in disgust. She pulled a bag out of her jacket and began popping what looked like nuts into her mouth.

Ember didn't reply. She was too busy reading the articles. They were all similar to the first—another award for excellent service in battle. Mario Nicholas Lucinello was a product of the flicker breeding program and was rarely seen in public. Some speculated whether he'd be the youngest flicker ever retired to Empyrean.

She scanned the list again, but none of the articles said anything about him going missing. Her heart soared as she realized he might not be her father after all. Then she brought the images up closer, and her shoulders slumped. The man was unmistakably a younger version of Dai. He didn't face the crowd proudly as a military hero would. Instead, he positioned himself behind his leaders, always turned away from the camera. That fit him as well. He'd never been a sociable man.

"Hey," Mar said. "I think I've heard of this guy. He was famous twenty years ago, right?"

Ember barely heard her. At the very bottom of the list was a film sequence. She clicked on it, then sat back to watch.

Dai—or Mario—stood atop a grand platform, looking down on a huge crowd. People shouted at him from down below. Commander Kane walked out and raised his arms. He called something out to those beneath him, and the crowd erupted in anger. Guards surrounded the people, Ember realized now, shoving them even closer together, herding them.

Kane lowered his arms and took a step back. His expression was murderous. He turned to Mario and said something under his breath.

Mario pressed his eyes shut, but he nodded. A deep breath, and then the screams began.

Ember hit Exit and stared at the screen in shock for a long moment.

It was true. Dai was a flare, the only documented person in

history who could do what Ember could. The knowledge was supposed to make her feel better, but somehow she just felt worse. He hadn't resisted at all.

He hadn't even worn a collar.

Mar looked sick, a nut half chewed in her mouth. She swallowed it and rose to her feet. "Uh, that was disturbing. Did he just —just do what I think he did?"

"*Stars,*" a girl said behind them. "I knew it was her. Hey, Peter, the assassin's sitting right here."

A group had assembled at the booth's opening. Most of the visitors kept their distance, but one pushed his way through and folded his arms. "Yep, it's her."

Ember stood as well, facing him. "Did you just call me an assassin?"

"Well, yeah. That's what you are, right? We all saw what you did this morning."

"What is he talking about?" Mar muttered.

"You must've just gotten here if you haven't seen it yet," he said to Mar. "Everybody in three galaxies has seen it multiple times."

"It?" Ember repeated, her stomach plummeting.

The guy went to the screen and swiped a few times. Then he pulled up an article with a dark-blue star. "Want to see it again, guys?"

"Yeah," a few of the group said, although most of them fidgeted uncomfortably.

The film sequence began. A reporter with blue hair and a long face like Talon's announced breaking news in Common. The Empire had just deployed nearly half its forces to an undisclosed location. Sources said they had received a tip about the Union's newest location and officials were determined to end the war once and for all.

"It has also been confirmed that the Empire has a secret weapon," the man continued. "It could quite possibly be the rise of not a flicker, but—get this—a *flare*. If it's true, the emperor's victory over the Union is assured."

Then the scene shifted, and Ember felt her throat tighten. A small ship surrounded by several others. It had been edited to look darker, more sinister than it really was.

Then a girl with dark-black hair, looking stern.

A shot of the woman crumpling to the floor. Another shot of herself, appearing determined and focused. The man slumping over the controls. Commander Kane's smug smile.

The reporter continued to talk, but Ember was on her feet. She stabbed the screen off and whirled to face the group, who stared back at her like deer frozen in a hunter's scope.

The Empire had edited out everything. The couple's peaceful surrender. Her screaming on the floor, the man's cries and promises for vengeance. Kane's kick to her ribs. She had a massive black bruise under her shirt because of it.

Mar was standing too, looking very much like the others. It was an expression all too familiar to Ember now, one she should have seen in Stefan when she first entered. Shock. Horror. Revulsion.

The entire ship knew about her now. If that man was right, several galaxies did. The only reason this video would have leaked was because the Empire wanted it to. Kane hadn't meant to keep her a secret for long. He wanted to intimidate the Union, make them surrender upon their arrival. Had Amai seen this too? Was their deal completely off now? She could imagine the Union ordering the ship's destruction any minute now, relieved they'd managed to kill the dangerous "secret weapon" before it reached them. This video could very well have sentenced them all to death.

Ember was breathing hard now. "It said half our forces were mobilized," she said to the staring group. "Where will the battle take place?"

Everyone looked at each other as if she'd asked them a question in Romani.

"Oh," Mar said, her voice wobbly. "I was going to tell you tonight sometime. Um, I overheard it at the station before they sent me here."

"Tell me what?"

"The Union made Earth their new base. The emperor has sent us to destroy every last trace of them."

Minutes later, Ember found herself in her quarters. She remembered pushing through the staring people on the rec deck and glimpses of reckless sprinting through the hallway, but there was too much on her mind to care how she'd looked to the others. Everyone knew what she was now.

Everybody but Ember.

It made sense now. She couldn't believe she hadn't put it all together before. The Union had her father at their camp because they were stationed nearby. They'd probably chosen Earth because it was abandoned and barely habitable. And they knew the Empire was aware of their location. Why else would Amai insist on blowing up this particular ship? If she could take out a high commander and a dozen trained flickers in one blow, that would be a huge victory indeed.

Ember lay on her bed, staring up at the high ceiling. Her stomach was doing a strange dance with that awful alcohol burning in it. The drink had begun to take effect, giving her a faint buzz along the edges of her mind, making it hard to focus.

Ember's choices were limited. If she somehow escaped and made it to Earth before the Empire did, she wasn't likely to survive the Empire's attack. But if she stayed, Kane would make her relive that public execution film sequence all over again.

Probably on an even more massive scale. She'd be killing the very people trying to keep her father safe.

She thought about that man, the one she had killed today. Or had she? His light had still been there, and that movement in his hand . . . Could it be that she'd found a way to knock a person unconscious without killing them? If only she could access the ship's records to find out what happened to the shuttle after Kane's little demonstration.

There was a soft knock on the door.

"Lock door," Ember commanded.

"I heard that," Mar called through the metal. "I know you're upset, but can I come in? I just need to ask you something."

Fine. "Open."

The door slid open. Mar entered silently and plopped herself onto the floor across from Ember's bed.

This was where people usually did one of two things—judge Ember or try to use her. If that was why Mar had come, she'd order her out immediately. "Well?" Ember said after a moment of silence.

Mar ignored Ember's impatience. "It wasn't like that video, was it?"

Ember turned her head to examine her friend. Mar's eyes were serious, any hint of her earlier smile gone. Her question seemed sincere. "No. It wasn't like that at all."

"I thought so. He forced you, didn't he?"

She wanted to say yes, but it wasn't completely true. He'd given her two lives and asked her to choose. Ember wasn't a god. It wasn't her right to save one life over another, just like it shouldn't have been her right to take lives. And yet here she was. Despite all she'd done, all her struggles, she was exactly where the stars predicted she would be, making exactly the wrong choices.

*Stars, take it from me,* she pleaded. *I don't want it. I never wanted this.*

"I heard you killed your attacker in phase three," Mar said. "Was that when you figured out that you could do . . . whatever it is you do?"

No. She'd discovered it at age sixteen, when she accidentally killed her own mother.

She could see herself kneeling over her mother's body and weeping as her father came in. She had no idea what she'd done. Dai could have explained it to her then. Why hadn't he? Was that the moment he knew exactly what his daughter was, or were the signs apparent much earlier?

"Stefan said he could see images in the light," Ember whispered. "But he doesn't actually touch the light. Is that how it is for you?"

Mar nodded. "Are you saying you can? Touch it, I mean."

Ember sat up and wrapped her arms around her knees. "Yes. I just reach out, and it feels real to me. As real as anything I've touched with my fingers." Maybe that was the key. Gripping the light and pulling removed the very soul from a person's body. Delivering a blow to that man had felt very different.

"Holy galaxy," Mar breathed. "I didn't even know that was possible."

"I answered your questions. Now it's your turn to answer mine." Ember rested her chin on her knees. "Why does the Empire hate the Union so much?"

Mar stared at her incredulously. "That's not a question you ask on an Empire carrier, especially with a high commander on board. All you need to know is they're the enemy."

"But what do you know about them? And I don't mean what the Empire force-feeds everyone. I mean facts. Who started the Union? What are they trying to accomplish?"

Mar sighed. "You aren't going to shut up about this, are you?"

"Nope."

"This is all I can tell you," Mar said in a hushed whisper. "The Union markets themselves as these honorable planet defenders, but that's not true. They're the ones attacking Empire planets, Ember. The Union leader is the emperor's daughter. She displeased the emperor one day, so he banished her. Now she's trying to take his throne for herself and using Union forces to do it."

"The Daughter," Ember muttered.

"Is that what they call her? Funny. You'd think they'd be a bit more original." Mar shrugged. "I don't have anything against them, personally. They're just doing what their crazy leader tells them to do. Same thing we're doing here."

"If you could end it," Ember said thoughtfully, "as in end the entire war, would you? If it meant taking lives?"

"That would require wiping out one side or the other. Since they're both fighting for the same position, I don't think that would change our situation much." Mar pursed her lips. "Do you have a plan?"

"I think I might." She turned toward the window again. They had picked up speed now. The stars barely moved as she watched, but the constellations changed every few hours. "But I'm going to need your help."

# 24

Three-and-a-half days. That was all the time Ember had to plan the end of a war.

Everything was different now. She couldn't walk anywhere without being recognized. People whispered when she passed them in the halls. They gave her a wide berth in any room. Even her instructors stopped calling on her, apparently choosing to ignore her rather than antagonize the creepy killer gypsy. In one ten-minute block of time, Commander Kane had separated her from everyone else. It wasn't hard to see herself the way they saw her—cold, heartless. An assassin.

She would have given anything to return to Eris's racial jabs at her people. It was far better than this.

Her classes and training sessions with Talon were put on hold for now. Her guard disappeared, leaving her to roam the ship alone. For a while it seemed as if Kane had forgotten all about her. Or maybe he knew she lived in a cage of her own making. The entire ship was her guard. They all knew where she was at any given time.

The atmosphere was unusually subdued on the last evening of their journey. Ember wolfed down her dinner and exited quickly, intending to spend the night in her quarters as usual. Mar was supposed to meet her there soon, hopefully with some new information she'd gleaned from her shift today. Earth was hours away now, and Ember still didn't know what to do.

"Ember," Stefan called out. He'd followed her out of the cafeteria.

"I don't have time to talk right now," she said with a forced smile. *I have to figure out how to save your life.*

He ignored her brush-off. "So you're a flare. That explains a lot."

A new pin decorated his collar today. He'd graduated from his training, whatever it was.

"Congratulations," she muttered. "Where's your assignment?"

"They want me to head the new 'Battle Anticipation Department.' Fancy way of saying they opened up a new division for the graduated flickers. Apparently it's hard to find good leadership there. Everyone wants to be the star, but nobody wants to do the work."

"I bet your family is very proud." She tried to imagine Stefan heading a group, calling out orders that meant the death of hundreds. It didn't seem to fit him.

Stefan's face darkened. "Actually, I'm not on speaking terms with my parents just now."

"Oh?"

"My grandmother died in prison last night. Mom called to tell me today. She said her mother deserved it after hiding from the Empire so long."

"Oh, Stefan." Ember nearly reached for him before remembering herself. She stilled her hands at her sides. "I'm so sorry."

He examined her for a long moment. "You are, aren't you?"

"I know how it is to lose someone."

He nodded. "The others pretend, but they don't understand. My grandmother practically raised me. She's the only one who asked me what my goals were instead of telling me, you know?"

He fingered the pin on his collar. "She was disappointed that I was fine with the life of a flicker. She wanted more for me."

"Ten hours to battle stations," an automated voice said over the speaker. "Ten hours."

*So soon.* Ember rubbed at the ache settling in her forehead. She'd looked forward to getting home for so long. Yet every minute that passed, she felt something heavy and sharp sitting in her stomach. She had to stop the Empire's attack somehow. But how could one person take down an entire fleet?

"You're upset," Stefan said. "Let me walk you to your quarters, if that's where you're going."

Ember nodded, not daring to speak right now. They started slowly down the corridor, side by side.

"You know," he said thoughtfully. "I'm still not sure what to think, Ember. I've seen so many sides of you. That first day at the market when you were in your element, you chewing me out when you woke up on the shuttle, watching you see the station with fresh eyes—it reminded me of when I first arrived as a kid, when everything was new and exciting."

She remembered too. It hadn't been that long ago, yet everything was different now.

"Then you progressed so quickly, and the big bombshell with you being a flare. I didn't know who you were anymore. I told myself you'd changed. But it wasn't you who changed, was it?"

He cut off as someone walked by. When he finally continued, his voice was barely audible.

"I always dreamed of becoming a special assistant to High Commander Kane. Pretty much all his assistants become somebody eventually. I longed for the realm to know my name. And then you came along and accidentally became everything I wanted to be." He chuckled bitterly.

"Stefan—"

"No, let me finish, because I know what you're going to say. According to the Empire, my grandmother was a terrible person for hiding her gift when she could have used it to serve them. That one thing alone turned her own daughter against her. Everything else, the other 99.9% of her personality, didn't matter because my mom chose to see her through the Empire's lens. Because of that, my parents didn't even question the fact that Grandma was perfectly healthy and should have lived another decade."

"You think they killed her in prison."

He nodded. "I knew it immediately. So when I ended Mom's call, I took a step back from the Empire's lens and took a good look at my life."

"And what did you see?"

"You, mostly." Stefan shot her a teasing smile, which faded quickly. "No, really. My grandmother should have had the right to choose how she wanted to use her gift. I think if they'd forced her into training, she would have acted much like you."

Ember felt her cheeks warm. "Stefan, I know you mean well. But I'm not the girl your grandmother saw."

Stefan stopped and turned to face her. "Forget about the vision. Forget about what Commander Kane and the other flickers and the emperor and everyone else wants. When I step away from the Empire's lens, I see a strong, independent woman who feels deeply for people and will fight to the last breath for those she loves. I see a woman who is fierce and mysterious and holds powers I can't even begin to understand." He took her hands in his, warm and strong. "I see a woman who will raise hellfire when she finally decides what she's doing next. And all I know is I want to be a part of it."

The very closeness of Stefan made her breathless. Was he really saying these words? She didn't dare hope.

Three more corners and she'd reach her quarters. Part of her wanted to slow down so she could maximize her time with Stefan. Another part was screaming to get away, to escape before she became even more entangled than she already was. "I'm not sure what you want me to say."

"My point is this, Ember. I don't know what your future is. I haven't read it, and I don't know if my grandmother did either. But it doesn't matter what the stars say. I read this quote from an Earthen writer once that said, 'The only person you are destined to become is the person you decide to be.'"

*The person you decide to be.* Not the person she was told to be or saw herself being in a vision. His words reminded Ember of something her mother had said the night after Ember refused Babik's proposal, just hours before her mother's death.

*Mother sat at the table across from Ember, frowning. She held a cup of green coffee in one hand. She always drank it when her illness got really bad, whether in the morning or at bedtime. Tonight was particularly bad—redness tinged her eyes, and she coughed every other sentence. She gripped the hot drink like a tether holding her to the ground.*

*"I don't care for Babik," Ember had insisted. "He watches me like a bear eyeing a fish. He thinks I'm privileged just to catch his attention. When I speak, he interrupts and argues and insists he knows better."*

*"He is trying to impress you." She coughed again and took a long sip. "You could do worse than the chief's son. At least you would have plenty of food. And Arama is a kind soul, a good mother-in-law. She would treat you well."*

*"I don't love him."*

*Her mother took another thoughtful sip. "Love is a gadje notion, Ember, an excuse and an impossible dream. Here, it is duty and responsibility above all else. It will always remain so." She shrugged. "You just need to decide who you will be."*

The memory was so sharp, so real it gripped Ember's throat like a hand. She realized she'd stopped walking. A small, empty corridor jutted off to their right. She stepped into it and fell against a wall, breathing hard.

*Forget about what Commander Kane and the other flickers and the emperor and everyone else wants.*

*Decide who you will be.*

She was tired of being the nail driven by another force. Her father had already lived that life, and it had broken him. She would never serve the Empire that way again.

It was time to become the hammer.

"The Union is supposed to be sending a shuttle for me when the battle starts," she said. "At least that was the plan a few days ago. But I can't get on it until the ship is disabled. Better yet, the fleet. I just need to have the battle contained first."

"The entire *fleet*? But how are you going to do that?"

"Let me worry about it. I'll send a message when I have it all worked out."

He laughed, his grip on her hands tightening. "Nice try, but I'm helping you."

She hesitated. "This isn't something you just decide, Stefan. This means leaving your family, your friends. This is forever. And if the Empire catches you, they won't be kind."

"Probably not, but I'm willing to risk it."

She gave him a long look, but he seemed sincere. "How can you give up everything so quickly?"

"Ember," he whispered. "Do you really not see it?"

"See what?"

He took a step toward her. "I give you permission to read me. Look inside, and you'll see the truth." His cheeks reddened in a maddeningly adorable way. "Just a peek, though."

She plunged into his light before thinking about it. She shuffled through his memories, including the one with his grandmother, and found that he'd described it exactly as it happened. She went forward to their first meeting, saw his surprise, interest, then admiration. The warmth in her chest flared into something bright and hot, and she could barely contain the emotion she saw there. From admiration to warmth and affection, and then—something far deeper.

He loved her.

She pulled out, feeling her own cheeks flush at some of the thoughts he held about her.

He watched her expectantly, nervously. "Did you—" he began, but she didn't give him a chance to continue. She threaded her fingers into his hair and pulled him downward, pressing her lips to his.

She felt his smile against her mouth, his hands pulling her closer. His lips moved against hers, insistent, impatient, strong.

Someone walking by hooted, as if they were just another couple. Two soldiers about to embark on a battle. Just two people from completely different galaxies whose futures were forever intertwined.

She finally pulled away, gasping for breath, and rested her head on his chest. His heart hammered as fast as hers, and his breathing was hard, as if he'd just run a race. His arms tightened even more around her waist, and the thin fabric against her skin felt even more scandalous than usual.

"It's been torture keeping this to myself," he whispered. "I'm glad you know."

Ember glowed inside. She'd kissed a *gadjo,* yet she didn't feel any different. Well, that wasn't true. She felt remade, whole. Complete. The filthiness and betrayal she'd expected to feel were completely absent, instead replaced by a pulsing heat she'd never felt before.

*Love is a gadje notion.* If that were true, maybe she'd decide to switch over.

She began to close the distance between them again, eyeing his lips, but he placed a finger on hers. "As much as I'd like to continue this, I think we'd better discuss a plan. You do have one, right?"

She checked her wristband. Thirty minutes until her meeting with Mar.

"Come with me," she said.

# 25

"They always know," Kane snapped at one of his assistants. "How? They're always in formation when we arrive."

"I don't know, sir. I wish I did—"

"Oh, stop sniveling. Are we ready?"

"All soldiers at battle stations, sir."

Ember stood at the window again, but not in Kane's office. They were in a control room with a huge window and several screens positioned on the walls. Twenty other men and women sat at control panels throughout the room, all watching Kane expectantly.

But Ember wasn't concerned about them. Instead, she gazed out the window at the Union forces. It was easy to be impressed. Though the Union's array of ships wasn't uniform in size and the individual fighters couldn't be less than three decades old, they did seem well armed and prepared for battle. Anyone who could make Kane go on a rampage like this was a worthy foe.

And a worthy ally, in her case. At least for today.

"They've sent us a message in text, sir," a woman with headphones said. "Their leader requests an unarmed negotiation meeting."

"I bet she does," Kane muttered. "Foolish girl. Reply with an order to stand down and surrender."

"Yes, sir." She turned back to her panel.

Stefan was in his new department overseeing the new flickers and ensuring that what they saw got transferred to the weapons specialists. His part in the plan was simple and, Ember hoped, not too dangerous. Mar had installed a small stolen security mic in Ember's jacket, which was connected directly to Stefan. He would hear Ember's orders and execute them, making it look as if she had obeyed and leaving her free to complete her part in the plan. It didn't allow him to reply to her, but Ember hoped that wouldn't be necessary.

Mar had also managed to send an encrypted message to Amai by routing it through several other systems. It was risky, and there was no way for Amai to respond, but Mar seemed optimistic it had gone through. They'd requested that Amai bring a stolen Empire shuttle with an empty hold and wait away from the fighting. In just an hour and forty-five minutes, Ember, Stefan, and Mar would eject from the ship in an escape pod and find her.

Ember hoped the message would be enough to keep Amai from blowing up their ship with them still on board. She hadn't done it yet, which was a good sign.

Ember's role was the most dangerous of all. She would wreak as much havoc as possible to disrupt the Empire's offensive efforts. But she'd have to be subtle enough to slip under Kane's radar. Especially since he wanted her right by his side.

Another assistant was talking to Kane now, speaking quickly.

". . . more ships than expected, sir. Do your orders stand?"

"They mean to intimidate us, but they can't. We have something they don't." Kane stepped over to Ember and slid his hand along her neck, gathering some of her hair. She flinched at his touch, and he smiled. "Are you ready to show off our power, my gypsy?"

"Yes, sir." Just not in the way he expected.

He dropped her hair, but didn't move away. "Status, Leonard?"

"Armed and ready, sir."

"The floor is yours."

Leonard bowed, then began barking orders before he'd even straightened, and the room came to life as everyone scrambled to obey.

Kane squinted at the ships as he softly spoke to Ember. "I want you to look for a specific person. Their commander, a woman aged thirty-six. She'll be heavily shielded."

The Daughter. Of course Kane would seek her first. Ember didn't intend to kill her, but she scanned the ships, pushing ever farther. It was difficult to scan so many vessels at once. Pilots, mechanics, security, soldiers. Children. She flinched. There were families on some of the ships. They were frantically evacuating, but it was clear the Empire had caught them before they were ready.

"I don't sense her, sir," Ember said honestly. "She must be giving orders from afar."

"Her death would greatly accelerate this war, gypsy, perhaps save thousands of lives. Keep looking."

"Yes, sir."

"The first shot is off, sir!" a soldier cried out unnecessarily. The flash of light that burst from an Empire ship ahead was impossible to miss. The well-aimed shot slammed straight into a freighter at its weakest shield-point, and its side erupted in flames.

*It's begun, Stefan and Mar. Please be safe.*

"Look for their general, then," Kane told her. "Once he's dead, take out the captains. They employ sixteen per carrier and two on smaller vessels."

"General and captains. Yes, sir." Ember didn't want too many casualties on the Union side, but the lack of deaths would be suspicious as well. She hoped Stefan had gotten the message. He would focus the weapon room's efforts in trying to minimize Union damage.

The battle had begun in earnest now. Shots flew on both sides, explosions scattering debris like feathers at a pheasant hunt. Ember focused her attention on the decks below. She would have to avoid a systematic approach to her ship's destruction. It would be too obvious.

*Stars, forgive me for this.*

She tested a captain first, a particularly sour man who barked orders and physically attacked his soldiers when they didn't move quickly enough. She sent a blow to the man's hot, angry soul. It flickered, and for a moment Ember held her breath, watching it carefully. It dimmed but didn't go out.

Relieved, she released her breath, then went back to work.

She couldn't say how long it had been. Ember's face felt too warm; her uniform was soaked in sweat. Kane was relentless in ordering entire ships taken down. It had taken her nearly an hour to render an entire ship unconscious, something that enraged Kane. He screamed at her, threatened her, breaking her concentration.

He didn't know what else she'd done in that time.

She checked her wristband, surprised to see that nearly an hour and a half had already gone by. Ember had planned to sneak out while Kane was issuing orders, but the man remained at her side the entire time.

"Sir," an assistant cried from the back of the room. "There seems to be something poisonous on deck three. The entire deck is on the ground."

"Quarantine sequence," Kane snapped.

"Already initiated. Several teams are already down there testing. They can't detect anything unusual, sir, but it's spreading upward now. A third of deck four has already succumbed."

Kane was quiet. How many people per minute?"

"Sir?"

"I want to know how many of my soldiers fall each minute. Ask them."

The assistant relayed the question, waited nervously, then came back. "Between forty and fifty per minute."

Kane's face darkened, and he turned to Ember. Her heart nearly skipped a beat under his murderous gaze.

"Sir?" she asked, but he wasn't buying her act any longer.

With a growl, he yanked Ember by the collar. "You think to attack my ship, you filthy little traitor?"

She immediately reached out to his inner light—and found it locked away behind an impenetrable shield. "Of course not, sir. I'm obeying your orders."

Without releasing her, Kane addressed the assistant. "Call the medical bay. Ask if they've had an unusually high rate of officers fall in the past half hour."

The assistant complied, his face growing paler by the second. Finally he closed the call. "Yes, sir. Six captains and two lieutenants have fallen with no warning whatsoever."

"Perhaps the Union has a flare too, sir," Ember said quickly. "Surely you don't think—"

"I don't think, you rat. I know." He released her with a disgusted look and held the trigger so she could see it. "Forty to fifty at once. You've been deceiving me all along."

"Oh, I'm the liar?" Ember shot back. "You never intended to protect Earth." She felt along Kane's invisible shield, but the edges were insubstantial. It was like trying to grasp air.

"What the Empire does with its own land is no concern of yours."

"What you do with *my people* and *my home* is absolutely my concern!"

His fist slammed the trigger, and suddenly she was on her knees in agony. She gritted her teeth, refusing to give him the satisfaction of crying out.

He grabbed her arm and dragged her toward a door on the opposite side of the room as the pain tore through her insides. The specialists watched her struggle until the door slid closed. Only then did Kane throw her arm to the ground and release the trigger.

Ember trembled, but she forced herself to scan the dark room. It had to be Kane's quarters—tall and fancy and smelling dreadfully like him. Cupboards much like the one he'd kept the collar in lined the walls. He was opening one now. Kane retrieved a tiny black box, slammed the cabinet shut, then stalked toward her.

"Remember that machine you broke?" Kane said, his voice deadly. "It was a lengthy examination of that machine that made me realize I've been going about this the wrong way. Seeing what a flicker sees is slightly helpful. Collaring and torturing a flare into submission is one step further. But it still leaves too much power in your hands, and we can't have that. You've made that all too clear."

He knelt by her side as she pushed upward, struggling to rise. Her body still shook too violently, however, and she soon fell back down, breathing hard.

He brought his stunner to her head. "I'm going to adjust your collar now. Stunners are fatal at such a close range, so hold very still."

She was tempted to fight. Stars, she wanted to fight him even if it meant her death. But Stefan and Mar would be making their way to the lift about now, and they wouldn't leave without her. She had to get them to safety. "The emperor would be furious if you killed me."

He reached behind her head to the metal pressing against her spine. It sent a jolt of warning down to her toes. A few more adjustments and the device hung a little heavier than it had before. He pulled back and examined it.

"Unfortunately, we haven't been able to test it yet due to a lack of subjects." He smirked and rose to his feet again, aiming the stunner at her chest. "Now, stand by the window."

Ember tested his shield again. Stronger than ever. She managed to roll onto her side, then rise slowly to a sitting position as the room spun around her. Then she pushed slowly to her feet. Lights flashed outside the window as shots were exchanged. The Union seemed to be holding their own against the Empire's front line, but there were still plenty of Empire ships holding back. What were they waiting for?

He pointed at a ship outside the window, a large Union carrier. "I want that entire ship's occupants dead. Start with the pilots, then the engineers. I want it out of commission in two minutes."

"No, Kane. I will not kill for you again, now or ever."

"I hoped you'd say that." He clicked something in his hand and spoke into it. "Kill everyone on that ship now."

The collar on her neck began to burn. Her skin underneath singed and she began to smell burning flesh. But she was so frozen in shock she couldn't do anything about it. She watched as her internal arm reached up, then forward.

"Who's doing this?" she demanded.

"You. Or, rather, your inner light. It rebelled against my testing machine, but it seems to have taken quite nicely to my updated reader. It took a bit of tweaking to get the signal just right. That's why I had Talon tune it to you during your training."

Ember thought back to the thousands of push-up and sprinting sessions, to those moments when her body had seemed to move on its own. She'd assumed she was just on automatic, but maybe it had been something more.

She tried to pull her inner arm back, but it was as if she were completely disconnected, and before she knew it, she was grabbing hold of the collective lights on the ship, easily penetrating a few shields as if they were nothing.

"No," she hissed, but it was too late. She yanked them all out at once.

The dots of light in the distance flickered and died. Three hundred and sixty-four at once.

Her chest seized until it was impossible to breathe.

Commander Kane stood next to her at the window now, watching as if nothing had happened. "I call it the C.O.L.A.R. 2.0, or Compulsion of Light Anticipation Remote. It takes the decision out of your hands and places it in mine, where it belongs. If only I'd had this twenty years ago when the first flare was under my command." He turned to face her. "Can you imagine the type of power this brings? It almost makes me more powerful than the emperor."

The carrier's internal lights flickered now. Its emergency power would be turning on soon, which would have kept the thrusters steady for several more hours if it weren't stranded in the middle of a battle. Without its shields, the ship would easily be hit and destroyed before long.

"See?" Kane said, a strange eagerness in his voice. "Several hundred at once. With me at the helm, all your mental barriers are removed. Now do the next ship over. In fact, I'll point, and you kill."

*Three hundred and sixty-four.* Two-thirds the number of people in her village. She'd just killed them all at once, and she hadn't even meant to.

He pointed, and the collar heated again, painfully singeing her skin. She bit her lip to keep from crying out as her arm extended again, reaching for the lights flickering in the distance. As she made contact with the terrified occupants of the next ship, she detected several infants among them. Several of their escape pods had left without their maximum passenger load, leaving many of the most vulnerable behind.

It was done in seconds. Nearly four hundred that time.

Twelve children.

*Stars, please,* Ember pled. *You have to stop this.* She imagined herself running out of the room and escaping, but her feet seemed just as disconnected as her light. Kane seemed to have complete power.

Another ship. And another.

One by one, each vessel went dark. The fifth exploded within seconds, probably meaning she'd killed a mechanic in the middle of refueling or working on the power core. Kane was bouncing on his toes now, looking very much like a child on his birthday.

*I have the right to decide.*

He pointed again, and she extinguished a smaller ship. Eighty-nine that time. The collar burned so severely now she could barely focus on the scene in front of her.

Her friends had to be waiting near the escape pod by now. Mar could probably be convinced to leave without her, but Stefan never would. He would simply die with her.

That meant it was time to fight.

She tried to gain control of her light to check Kane's shield again, but it didn't even acknowledge her. Another ship went down—a smaller ship but with over two hundred passengers. A civilian ship.

Kane pointed again, this time to the largest vessel, which had just emerged from the planet's atmosphere. "There's the one. I've been waiting for her to show herself."

Her consciousness eagerly thrust out a hand in obedience. Ember left it alone, focusing all her concentration on Kane's shield. Then she summoned a second hand from her light. It flickered and moved slowly, but at least it was something. She probed Kane's shield, then began to beat it with her fist.

Kane's head jerked up, and his eyes narrowed. "You shouldn't be able to do that." He adjusted his trigger, then jabbed the button again. Red-hot agony swept through Ember, sending her writhing on the ground again, but this time she was prepared.

She closed her eyes and began to hum.

Her consciousness began to lose its grip. She was fading out.

She directed all her strength to the notes. Every last inch of herself, every cell that still existed, she sent to making the sounds. Burning with anger and pain, she opened her mouth and shouted the lyrics, the words all jumbled and barely coherent.

Then she summoned her second hand once more, feeling her inner light brighten to a feverish intensity.

All her frustration and pain and anger and determination swelled in her throat. She released one giant, final yell as she threw herself at the shield.

It smashed into a thousand pieces.

Kane's face went pale. "You can't—"

She grabbed the light.

And yanked.

The commander jerked, then dropped as if in slow motion, the trigger slipping from his hand and tumbling away as he hit the ground.

He released a last breath and went still.

Ember's pain stopped abruptly. The room closed in on her and she gave in to the precious blackness.

# 26

Ember awoke to a sensation of swaying. She forced her eyes to focus and stared uncomprehendingly at the corridor walls surrounding her. They were moving. Something tightened around her, a familiar smell penetrated her nostrils, and suddenly she felt very much at home.

"Just relax," Stefan said somewhat breathlessly. "I've got it all worked out." It was his arms around her. She recognized the feel of them.

"Stefan?" It came out as a whisper. Not responding, he stopped, looked around the corner, and resumed his long stride.

They reached a huge metal door. It felt significant somehow, this door. It was open. Stefan set her gently down on the floor. Mar smiled at her from above. "This is no time for sleeping, princess. Your chariot awaits."

"Halt!" a voice shouted from down the hall.

"Get her onto the ship, Mar," Stefan said quickly. "You'll make it if you hurry. The coordinates are already entered, but keep radio silence for the first ten minutes or so. Your ship is supposed to be unmanned. And make sure you get her to a medic, all right?"

"You there!" the guard called, closer now.

This was wrong. Panic welled up Ember's throat. "Stefan?"

His warm gaze settled on her. "I was meant to help you, Ember. That's exactly what I intend to do."

"No," she whimpered, sitting up. It was all coming back. "I'm not going without you."

"Yes, you are." He slammed his fist on the Close button, and the door began to move.

"Doors closing," an automated warning announced. The escape pod.

The guard stopped and took aim, but Ember punched his inner light as she'd done with the others, sending him tumbling to the ground. She struggled to her feet, legs shaking, and searched for a button to stop the doors from closing. "There's got to be another way. We can figure this out."

The doors continued to close. Only Stefan's upper half was visible now. "I tried to disarm the theft feature, but it didn't work. It has to be done manually, from the corridor panel. You won't get far otherwise."

"Absolutely not. I won't leave without you."

He sent her a pleading look. "Trust me, Ember. This is exactly what my grandmother said would happen. It's an honor to make this sacrifice for you."

"Stefan—" She tried pulling the doors back, but they were too strong. Her body trembled too violently to try and leap through. She could barely support her own weight.

"Don't. This is what the stars decreed, Ember. I just wish we could have been together in the end."

He reached in, grabbed her face, and kissed her fiercely. He pulled away at the very last second, jerking his head and arms back just in time.

She reached for him. "Please, don't do this!"

But the giant door closed with a huge metallic *clang.*

Then silence.

Ember threw herself at the door and began to pound on it, but Mar grabbed her arm. "You can't open it now. Safety feature. C'mon, we can still make it if we hurry. Once they stun Stefan, we're on our own." She pulled Ember into the pod and clasped Ember's harness as if she were a parent buckling a small child in for safety.

*Stefan.* She still felt the warmth of his kiss on her lips. This wasn't how it was supposed to happen. The stars had brought them together.

"Initiating," Mar said, and the door closed just as the pressure changed outside of the craft. "Launching in three, two . . ."

Shouts on the other side of the door made Ember tear at her harness, but it was too late to turn back now. She sensed three lights confronting Stefan and ripped them out, leaving him alone. She could do that much for him at least.

Ember had left a huge part of herself on the other side of that door. And now the Union was going to blow up the ship, and Stefan with it.

"Maybe if we find Amai quickly, we can try to change her mind," Mar said, obviously trying to cheer her up. "Or maybe even postpone it until the other ships are down. I mean, you already killed the commander, so what's the rush?"

They spent several long minutes silently staring out the window as the Empire carrier grew smaller behind them.

Ember craned her neck to keep the vessel within sight as long as possible. If she locked her gaze on it and refused to let go, nothing could happen to it.

*Stefan*—such an idiotic, frustratingly courageous thing for him to do. He'd been so firm about his grandmother's theory and his role in her supposed quest. Stefan was so much like Dai in that way. *The stars are never wrong.*

But Ember wasn't the girl Stefan thought she was. That alone was proof that the stars didn't direct her future. *She* did. And she refused to sit back and watch Stefan die.

Ember closed her eyes, let her body relax, and reached out internally. The lights began to appear in clusters. She drew closer until she could distinguish one side from the other. Then she focused her attentions on Stefan's ship, searching for Amai's friends. Her heart hammered wildly in her chest with each second that passed. This was taking too long. It would take precious minutes to find them and stop their terrible mission.

She released a long, focused breath. Then she sent a blow toward the entire ship at once.

It was like fanning a flame. Hundreds of lights lit up brightly for a moment, then went low. A few flickered out, but most wavered only slightly. She hoped Stefan was one of the latter.

Ember worked on several more ships, rendering the occupants unconscious. Two Union vessels noticed the Empire ships' odd courses and prepared to fire, but Ember had prepared for that possibility. She sent them a light blow, hoping the other Union ships would get the message.

They seemed to understand. Amazingly, the front line broke as the fighters pulled back. And even more remarkable was a sight Ember hadn't dreamed she'd ever see.

The Empire ships were retreating.

Waves of people were dropping at once, hundreds per Empire ship. Ember could sense their terror from here. The fallen would return to consciousness eventually, but the battle would be over by then. She had created a temporary halt to the war.

"Amai," Mar said into the radio, eyeing Ember with a smile. "There's been a change of plan."

# 27

"I still can't believe they left," Mar said, sipping a nutrition packet. "The Empire never retreats."

They sat in a small gathering room in a temporary shelter not far from Ember's village—or what was left of it. Amai had refused to answer Ember's questions about her people, telling her to wait until a transport arrived and she could see for herself. She could barely sit still.

"It was ingenius, what you did," Amai said, smiling at Ember. "Although I'm not sure how long they'll stay away. We don't have much time."

Ember shifted in her chair, the packet in her hand untouched. She'd arrived happy to have Stefan alive, only to receive the worst possible news.

Dai was gone. He had died two days before. If Ember had left when Amai wanted her to, she could have said good-bye.

It left a hollow feeling inside of her, where her heart had once been.

"Your gravity is so *intense* here," Mar moaned. "And depressing. How did humans live on this planet for so long?"

"It wasn't always like this," Amai said. "I've seen photos."

Ember stood. "I want to see my village now."

"I've told you. We're just waiting for the transport."

"*You're* waiting for the transport. I'm walking." Ember jerked the door open and plunged into the heavy sunlight, which instantly warmed her in her thick black jacket. It was the most amazing feeling in the world.

The two women stared after her. "But it's six kilometers, and —" Amai said.

Slamming the door behind her, Ember missed whatever the woman was going to say next. She faced forward, noting the launchpad in the distance where tourist shuttles had once landed. No ships stood there now. Instead, a plume of white smoke rose lazily into the sky.

Just past that was the Roma market and her stall, she knew. And even farther beyond lay her village. Home. She was so close.

She began to run.

Ember knew the truth when she saw the market. Tables overturned, chairs destroyed. Blanket dividers torn and strewn about. Birds hopped around, exploring the empty market like it was a new playground. The most disturbing thing was the plastic shoes scattered on the ground. The shoemaker had left his wares behind. Not a good sign.

She put on a burst of speed and raced up the hill, but she already knew what she would find. Curls of lazy white smoke still rose from the top of it.

Her village was a smoking wreckage, its previous buildings now piles of rubble. Not a structure had been spared. They'd even downed the well house and kicked it to pieces. The worst of it began as she picked her way farther into the village among piles of rubble that were charred and black. She could barely tell where she was now.

Her boot brushed a misshapen log, and she stepped back to examine it, then recoiled in horror. A body. She couldn't tell by the shape whether it was a man or a woman. One arm protruded as though the poor soul had been reaching for something. Or someone maybe.

The Empire had swept through here with their gas torches, but it was hard to tell how long ago. The emperor had obviously seen Ember's village as a loose end, a possible breeding ground for flares. A threat that had to be eliminated now that the Empire was near. Not people but liabilities.

A game piece that had to be swept off the board.

Her feet moved of their own accord to where her home had once stood. Just like everything else, it was a pile of charred material. She could still see it there in spirit—its narrow doorway to the right with the broken window. The courtyard to the left. Her hens clucking their welcome as she stepped inside. The table her father had so meticulously carved with flowers on its legs. Her family's image frozen forever in a stained-glass frame. It existed only in her mind now.

She scrambled to the pile, fell to her knees, and plunged her hands into the wreckage. She tore a broken piece of wood off the top and threw it, then another. Her arms grew weary as she worked frantically through the pile, searching for what she knew she would never find.

"Your father's body was buried with the others," Amai said as she stepped out of the transport behind her. Mar sat with a stunned expression, her eyes down. There was no driver. "He died in our shelter. I promised you we would protect him as best we could."

Ember stood, her knees sore from the sharpness of the debris beneath her. "And yet he's dead."

"He was sick, far beyond our help. I daresay he was beyond anyone's help. Your being here wouldn't have changed anything."

"You're wrong! I was getting him medicine. He would have

pulled through. I know it." She kicked a piece of metal and winced when it didn't budge.

"He showed us his pill bottle. It wasn't the right kind, Ember. The medics think he had cancer, and your medicine was for pneumonia."

"It was helping. I know it was."

She sighed. "There's something else." Amai stepped down from the vehicle and approached Ember, handing her a square device. "This is really what we were waiting for, not the transport. I wanted you to see it first, but . . ." She shrugged. "Anyway, this seemed really important to him. Just tap the screen."

Ember reverently fingered the tablet. Her father's face was frozen in a smile, much like the stained-glass image of him. But here his eyes looked sunken and oversized, his skin sallow. He barely looked like himself except for the smile. Could he have changed that much in three weeks?

She tapped the screen, not daring to breathe.

"My dear Ember," her father said in Common, grinning. "If you're watching this, I'm dead. It's easy enough for me to accept because I knew this was coming, but I know it will be difficult for you. There's so much I want to say and not nearly enough time to say it. I need several more years, I think." His grin faded, and he swallowed.

Ember covered her mouth with one hand, her throat tightening.

"I know what happened to you. It's what I feared all along and couldn't stop. I should have taken you away, hidden you far from the Empire's reach. But you seemed content enough, so I let myself believe embracing Roma life might hide you better than any cave could. Forgive me. The Empire will do anything to capture and tame a wild flicker, especially someone with your unique skills. I should have done a better job protecting you, preparing you for what would come."

Ember felt her stomach drop. Dai wasn't talking about the Empire now. He was talking about her gift.

After Ember's mother died, her father's devastation was even harder to stomach than the crushing sorrow she'd experienced. He looked at her differently after that, keeping a wary sort of distance. But there had been something else in his eyes, something inward and very, very deep. Now she knew what it was. Guilt.

He knew his daughter was a flare. He hadn't seen it in her until it was too late, and because he'd failed to prepare her, his wife was gone forever. He blamed himself, not Ember.

"I escaped the Empire and ran to the safest place I knew," Dai continued. "Earth lies on the boundaries, still within the Empire's reach and jurisdiction but far beneath their notice. I thought I would be safe here, and I was for many years. I just didn't consider what it would mean for my daughter. I'm sorry."

He gestured to the camera. "These people, the Union fighters, are kind. They've taken good care of me. They allowed me to make this recording for you. I believe siding with them is a good decision."

Ember looked at Amai, who was listening with a frown.

Then her father switched to Romani.

*My Ember, when I say siding with the Union is a good decision, I only mean it is slightly better than serving the Empire. They mean well, but be wary of their leader. They call her the Daughter. She is the daughter of the emperor, cast out long ago for reasons unknown to me. If you choose to serve her, be very careful. I have yet to discover whether this Union is the antithesis of the Empire or an extension of it.*

*Good-bye, my light. I look forward to watching you grow from the stars.*

*I can't tell you in words how I feel for you. It was the greatest pleasure of my life to be your father.*

He motioned to whoever held the camera, and then it went black.

Ember found herself clinging to the tablet in her hands, holding it so tightly she feared it would break. She forced herself to loosen her grip and tapped the screen again, watching it several more times until Amai cleared her throat.

"I'm sorry, Ember," she said. "But it's time to evacuate. Most of the other ships have left. I got special permission for you to say your good-byes first, but the Empire will be back *en masse*, and soon."

Ember gave her village one last look, then climbed into the transport, gripping her father's message firmly in both hands.

"What was that language your father spoke?" Amai asked as the transport moved. "And what did he say?"

"Romani," she said softly. Was Ember the last person who spoke their language? The realization made her physically ache. "He said it was a pleasure to raise me as his daughter."

Amai looked a bit suspicious, but she finally nodded.

They headed back to the camp, Ember's gaze locked on her feet the entire way. She folded her arms, feeling the strongest pieces of herself crumbling like the buildings around her, and she tried desperately to hold herself together before she fell completely apart.

A ship now stood a hundred meters from the temporary shelter she'd evacuated over an hour before. Workers were taking down the tents and loading the ship with boxes. The shuttle reminded Ember of the one that had whisked her far away from home and clinched her people's terrible deaths. Did they blame her, wherever they were now? Was her father right? Could they watch her from the stars?

She boarded and found a seat. Then she gasped. The woman sitting in the seat across from her was Bianca.

She launched herself across the aisle and embraced her friend, giving her a quick peck on the cheek. "Bianca! You're alive!"

Her friend stiffened, then pushed Ember away, her expression murderous. "Don't touch me."

"But—" Ember looked around. Bianca's son and husband were nowhere to be found, and her stomach looked a bit flatter. "No."

"They killed Gavril and my Luca. Shot them down in seconds. The shock of it was too much. The baby came shortly after—" She sucked in a sob. "It was a girl."

"Oh, Bianca."

"Don't pretend like you had nothing to do with this, Ember. I wish your filthy *gadjo* father never came to our village at all." Her friend removed her harness and stomped to the next passenger area.

Ember watched her go, feeling her heart sink to her toes.

Mar stood in the doorway. She cleared her throat. "Um, Amai asked me to give you this. The Daughter wants to speak with you, but not in here." She motioned to the door.

She followed Mar into an empty storage compartment on the ship. For the second time that day, Ember held a tablet in her hands. She tapped the screen as Mar left the room.

A woman not much older than Ember and dressed in white appeared, frowning at her. "Ember, daughter of Mario Nicholas Lucinello. I had hoped to speak with you before now, but alas, events have made that impossible." Her mouth tightened in what was probably intended to be a smile. "Is it true you are a flare?"

Ember recalled her father's warning about his woman. She did seem rather direct, like the daughter of an emperor would be. "I am."

Her lips tugged upward for a fraction of a second. "You are determined to join the Union against the Empire?"

"Yes." There was no doubt in her voice this time.

"We've recruited soldiers from all over the realm, Ember, but your role will be far more important. You will not train with them or climb their ranks. You will serve under me and me only. That requires absolute trust. Will you submit to a reading when you arrive?"

The Daughter wanted another flicker to comb through her memories to ensure she wasn't a double agent. She had nothing to hide except a tinge of doubt planted in her by Dai. Determination swelled within her as she made her decision. She would take the Empire down. If this woman became a part of it, she would take her down too. "I will if you'll do the same."

The woman's expression froze, then her calm demeanor returned. "I regret that isn't possible. You understand why the Daughter can't be read by a flare, particularly one who is yet untested. Perhaps someday."

Ember nodded. "I agree to your terms, then, on a different condition. There is a man on the ship I left. A prisoner."

"Ah yes. The usual request. Give your escort a description of the man, and we'll add him to the list. Our flickers will search for him. Hopefully we can get him out before his vessel is destroyed."

It was as far from a promise as the woman could make, but Ember pushed away her irritation. It was better than nothing. There was no way she could waltz onto the ship and save Stefan herself, not when the entire Empire was looking for her. "Fair enough."

"Good. Then we'll see you when you arrive. I look forward to working with you." The screen went dark.

Her father's words still streamed through her mind as she made her way back to her seat. The room's occupants began murmuring as she reentered the hold, but she barely noticed.

Ten minutes later they left Earth's atmosphere. Ember was surprised to see that Mar was right—their ocean was a murky brownish-blue from above. Her world may be imperfect, but it was hers. *I'll return someday,* she promised.

Forty minutes later the planet was a tiny dot in the window. Deep in thought, Ember kept her gaze on it until it disappeared completely. What would service in the Union mean for her? Was she switching from one enemy to another? Would they really help Stefan escape, or did they just want her badly enough to say anything she wanted to hear? Was Stefan's grandmother right about her—would she shape the universe around herself somehow?

*The only person you are destined to become is the person you decide to be.*

She turned to see the other passengers dozing. Bianca and Mar were somewhere on this ship as well, finally safe. She wouldn't rest until Stefan was back at her side, where he belonged. And then she had some serious work to do.

"I don't care anymore, stars," she said. "It doesn't matter why you gave me this gift, because my life is not your choice. It's mine. And now that I've made my decision, I will never apologize again."

THE END

EMBER'S STORY CONTINUES APRIL 2018

PREORDER FLARE - Only 99¢ for a limited time!

Visit http://books2read.com/flare to reserve yours today.

## A MESSAGE FROM THE AUTHOR

**Want two free books?**

Join my reader's club at http://smarturl.it/ClanVIP. It's fast, easy, and you get some serious deals and free stuff. I'd love to see you there!

If you liked what you read, please consider leaving a review. It helps greatly in spreading the word.
THANKS FOR READING!

## EXPERIENCE THE AWARD-WINNING DYSTOPIAN SERIES FOR 20% OFF

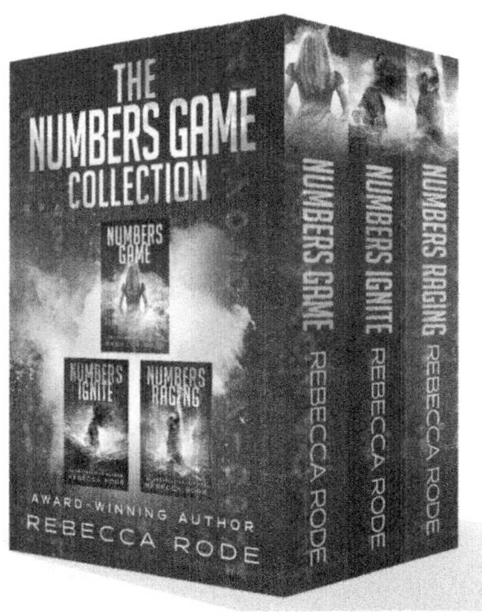


Everyone wore a number. That number represented everything about us. The rating was everything—until we discovered what was really going on.

Visit http://www.authorrebeccarode.com/numbers-game-collection/ to save $3 on the boxed set!

# ACKNOWLEDGMENTS

It's always scary to switch genres, but I had some seriously amazing helpers to get me through. Thanks to Gwynn White and the other Dominion Rising authors for the amazing ride. I learned things I never thought possible and made some great friends along the way.

Special thanks to my critique partners, Lindzee Armstrong, LaChelle Hansen, Darren Hansen, Nichole Eck, Adrienne Monson, Karen Pellett, Ruth Craddock, Roxy Haynie, Angela Brimhall, Mary King, Jen Greyson, and Karyn Patterson. You guys took my rough materials and helped me shape a cohesive story, and I appreciate it. I also have to thank Janci Patterson, Megan Walker, and Emily Christensen for joining us at the cabin for a writing retreat. You ladies helped me keep my sanity and get this thing done. Someday I want to be more like you.

Thanks to Clarissa Yeo with Yocla Designs for the amazing cover design, as always, and to Michele Preisendorf from Eschler Editing for her spectacular and speedy line editing. Michele not only squeezed me in before her family vacation, but she went above and beyond with her feedback—and I love her for it!

And I appreciate beta readers Adrienne Monson, Roxy

Haynie, Karen Pellett, Angela Brimhall, and Jen Greyson for getting through Flicker in the five days I allotted them (in the middle of summer, no less) and still giving me amazing feedback. They're still talking to me, so hopefully they weren't too traumatized.

I have to acknowledge my fantastic proofreading team as well, including Deshanna Harrison, Johanna Halbrooks, Lisa Carstens, Robyn Rudd, Nicole Davis, and Mary King (who caught the typos everyone else missed). These ladies had two days to scour Flicker for mistakes, and they rose to the occasion beautifully.

And finally, to my readers. Thanks for your patience, your unfailing support, and your help in spreading the word. This would all be pointless without you. Thanks for everything.

# ABOUT THE AUTHOR

REBECCA RODE is the USA Today and Wall Street Journal best-selling author of the Numbers Game series, the Ember in Space series, and numerous novellas. She also dabbles in freelance journalism, producing articles for Deseret News, KSL.com, and the Provo Daily Herald. She has four children, two cats, one husband, and a ridiculous number of books. Visit her at www.AuthorRebeccaRode.com.

Visit her at www.AuthorRebeccaRode.com or join her VIP Clan to get two free books: http://smarturl.it/ClanVIP

## ALSO BY REBECCA RODE

Numbers Game

Numbers Ignite

Numbers Raging

Chan's Story

Ruby's Story

Richard's Story

Love Right: A Sweet Romance Novella